Ghosts from the Veil

Five Detective Hugh McRath Supernatural Mysteries

Scott Williamson

Ghosts from the Veil

To Kirsten and our clan.

Contents

Introduction

Edinburgh is in my bones. I have lived here all my life and couldn't imagine being anywhere else; it is only right that it feeds so much of the stories I write.

I often walk up the Royal Mile in the centre of Edinburgh, through the narrow passageways of the Old Town and around Edinburgh Castle (and maybe stop at the odd pub for a pint and a few chapters of a book if I am being honest) just letting the history of my city seep into my chest. Often on these walks I think about the thousands of regular people who have tread the same streets, going about their lives but in a different period—thousands of stories wrapped up in the city's history. How interesting would it be to have a conversation with some of the past residents of Edinburgh just to understand what life was really like for them?

It was on one of my walks Detective Hugh McRath was born. I imagined him hobbling his way up the Royal Mile like I do—only he was in a grumpier mood. As he walked up the Royal Mile with the help of his cane, I saw him staring down at a peculiar watch, with multiple different hands, none of which were telling him the time. I thought, wouldn't it be cool if he was going to meet someone from the past and the watch was pointing him in their direction? A lost ghost, a spirit who used to stalk the same streets as I do on my walks. That was when the idea was born—a supernatural detective, who helped the ghosts of Edinburgh pass across the veil back to the land of the dead.

I grew up reading grumpy Scottish detectives and, if I'm being honest, surrounded by foul-mouthed grumpy Scotsman in general, so it was natural for Hugh to be the same. He just flowed out of me, annoyed and swearing at the ghosts who were interrupting his retirement from the police. But the man also has a heart and feels a responsibility to help the lost souls.

The ghosts may need his help, but Hugh also needs help, which is where his accomplice Fanny Archibald comes in. She is a ghost herself, here to help Hugh send the lost souls back across the veil. I thought it would be fun for Fanny to be someone Hugh found particularly annoying, which is why she is a well-spoken teenager. She was born in 1850 and murdered in 1865 but doesn't want to cross back over to the veil, as she would much rather spend her time with Hugh— much to his frustration. The dynamic of Hugh and Fanny is the part I enjoy the most when writing their stories.

There are five stories in this collection. Each story is about a different ghost (or ghosts) who Hugh and Fanny must help back across the veil by understanding why they are visiting the land of the living. All five stories are set in Edinburgh and inspired by the feeling the city gives me when I wander her streets. I hope you have as much fun reading the stories as I had writing them.

Scott Williamson
Edinburgh, Scotland

Swimming with the Past

Detective Hugh McRath was sweating. Not the sweating which caused a delicate dribble down the side of your temple. No, this was the type which left dark patches the size of continents under each arm and a puddle of water in the crack of your arse.

He shifted uncomfortably on the plastic seat he was melting into, his weight causing the chair to groan in complaint. Up in the stands at the side of the Royal Commonwealth Swimming Pool the air was sticky, stifling and reeked of chlorine.

Hugh glanced down at his watch. It was a peculiar watch, gold faced with three hands—none of which were telling the time. One spun round at a constant rate, telling him there were supernatural beings somewhere close by. That was nothing new—this was Edinburgh after all, the supernatural were everywhere, you couldn't move without bumping into the spooky bastards.

The second hand on his peculiar watch pointed towards the swimming pool and had done since he left his flat. Hugh had limped his way from Edinburgh's Old Town up to the Commonwealth pool (otherwise known as the "Commie") leaning on his cane as he walked, grumbling and stumbling in the direction the second hand on his peculiar watch pointed.

The third hand was currently dormant. Hugh would prefer it to stay that way.

As he frowned down at his watch, a bead of sweat took advantage of the extra momentum to enjoy a roller coaster ride down his wrinkled forehead before settling in his bushy grey eyebrows.

How could he be sweating this much just sitting still? He really needed to partake in more exercise than his nightly walks to the pub and the zig zagging stagger home. It was hardly enough to keep a fat bastard, who was creeping ever closer to sixty, in shape.

Maybe he should have brought his swimming trunks. That would have cleared the pool out pretty quickly. Him, his budgie smugglers, and distended belly making the kids scream and run for their mummies. He might have pulled off trunks back when he used to come here, but not anymore. The polis would be called as soon as he stepped out of the showers.

Hugh mainly remembered this place as the venue for his daddy and daughter days with Karen back when she was waist height. He could still picture her squealing with delight as she jumped into his arms in the pool. Did she do the same with his granddaughter now?

He shifted in his seat, the memory or the puddle in his underwear making it uncomfortable to sit still. His underwear squelched in response. His three-piece suit, bowler hat, and dark brogues were not exactly suited to the inside of a sweltering swimming pool. But Hugh didn't know how to dress down, no matter the occasion or temperature.

A family of four redheads sitting a few rows down were watching the divers throw themselves from the 10m board. The amateur fallers were hitting the water with varying degrees of satisfying plops and teeth grinding slams. The two young girls of the ginger family, being horrible children, had been cheering and giggling at the most painful belly flops.

Hugh wondered how funny things would be when whatever drew him to this sweatbox started kicking off. Not that he wanted anything to happen, of course—frankly, he could think of better ways to spend Saturday than investigating pissed off apparitions. Maybe sitting in a cold dark pub, devoid of screaming children, a cool pint of heavy sat in front of him as he watched the football results come in. Now that was how you spent Saturday.

Hugh licked his lips, tasting salt dripping from his thick bushy moustache which lay across his top lip like a wet dog. He lifted a red handkerchief from his top pocket (the one he'd chosen to match his tie and socks) and mopped his brow. The handkerchief quickly became heavy, so he rang it out on the floor between his legs, raindrops of his sweat pattering against the concrete.

"Delightful," whispered a scornful voice in his right ear.

Hugh jumped out of his seat, causing it to slam shut behind him as he fell to the ground, his bowler hat rolling into the row in front.

The two redhead kids from the family in front spun round to see the source of the commotion. When they spotted Hugh crumpled between two rows, the older of the two cretins pointed and giggled with the viciousness only a child could muster.

Hugh lifted his arm up and stuck his middle finger up at the two girls who immediately stopped giggling, their mouths falling open.

"How mature," came the voice by Hugh's side.

Hugh turned towards the whispery voice. Sat in the seat next to him was a teenage girl. Except she wasn't like any teenage girl of today's ilk. The blue tinge of a mobile phone screen didn't shine off her face for starters. Instead, all the colour in her looked faded like clothes which someone had put through too many washes.

She dressed in the style of her era. A black frock buttoned up to her neck and long enough to cover her feet. Not a piece of flesh on display except for her head—which was dripping with blood. The blood, almost grey in colour, came from a deep gash at the top of her forehead where someone had been kind enough to implant a butcher's cleaver back in 1865. The cleaver had been removed, but the wound remained open, deep, and constantly oozing down her face and dress.

Fanny Archibald. Born in Edinburgh in 1850. Murdered in the Old Town in 1865. A pain in Hugh's backside since 2018.

Hugh jabbed his cane at the girl, its tip passing straight through her and clattering against the chair she was sitting on.

Fanny gave him a bemused stare.

"Have I not told you how bloody creepy it is when you whisper in my ear?" grunted Hugh.

"Well, I thought as a supernatural detective you would be used to your partner appearing by your side by now."

She liked to think she was Hugh's crime solving partner, and in truth, she was the closest thing he had to a partner since his time on the police force. Or a daughter, if he was being honest, since his actual daughter would rather pull her teeth out with rusty pliers than speak to him.

But he wasn't about to tell Fanny either of those things.

"I told you, I am a detective, not a supernatural detective," he said, dragging himself back up to his feet, the arse of his trousers now feeling like a wet rag. He groaned as he leaned over to lift his bowler hat from the row in front. Repositioning the few strands of hair back across his balding scalp he placed the hat back on his head and sat down next to Fanny.

Despite the oozing gash in her forehead and her dying over 150 years ago, there was no stench drifting from her. Instead, Hugh had the usual metallic taste at the back of his mouth caused by the presence of the supernatural. That and the impending sense of doom. Both the taste and the doom he tried to remove at night with copious amounts of whisky.

"Since one helps ghosts and does not catch criminals, how can one say they are a detective?" asked Fanny.

"I wish *one* creepy bitch would leave me alone."

"And how would you deal with the dead in my absence? Would you just scowl them back across the veil to the land of the dead?"

"They can piss off as well."

"Oh, you don't mean that. I know there is a heart beating under all that blubber and grumpiness," said Fanny, a smug grin on her face, "why would you choose to help if there was not?"

Hugh frowned. "*I* had a choice in all this, did I? You sure fooled me."

Fanny waved a dismissive hand at Hugh, her dirty fingernails disappeared through his arm and out the other side. "Of course you had a choice. We always have a choice in life—I just helped you make the right one."

"A man is in no fit state on his deathbed to make the right choice."

But somehow, of all the deathbeds she could have chosen, this fifteen-year-old with a cleaver shaped wound in her forehead had appeared at Hugh's and convinced him to keep living.

Keep living, so he could help the dead.

Apparently, she thought helping the dead come to terms with what happened whilst they were alive would help him feel better about his own life decisions. Fanny hadn't factored in how many bad decisions Hugh had made in his life.

"Anyway. Stop being so grouchy. You are alive, aren't you? Unlike some of us," said Fanny.

Hugh grunted and licked his lips, tasting salt briefly on the tip of his tongue.

"You are alive and sweating—a lot."

"How observant of you Fanny."

She frowned. "You know I don't like being called that. It is Detective Archibald."

"Yeah, well, tough shit. You shouldn't have been born in a period when Fanny was an acceptable name to call your child."

She grumbled and scratched the gaping wound in her forehead.

"Stop picking that," said Hugh, "it's disgusting."

Fanny inserted a whole finger into the wound, a puckering squelching sound like welly boots in mud came from her touch.

Hugh gagged and turned away.

"Oh, I am sorry, is one creeping you out, detective?"

"Gee it a rest," said Hugh.

He glanced down at his watch; the shorthand was spinning faster than it had earlier. Was Fanny sat next to him causing his watch to get excited or was whatever called him to the swimming pool on a Saturday ready to make an appearance?

"Right, tell me, what's about to happen here?" asked Hugh.

"You tell me, you are the detective after all."

"And you are the fucking ghost."

"Supernatural being actually."

"Aye, very good. No, but seriously, what's about to happen?"

"Well, one is guessing something spooooooooky!" Her voice turned into a deep, bone chilling rattle, which made the hair on Hugh's neck stand up.

One of the girls in front of them spun in her seat and frowned towards Hugh and Fanny. She couldn't see Fanny, of course, only Hugh had that pleasure. But kids, even little shit kids like this one, knew more about what was going on around them than adults.

Hugh grinned at the little girl, then stuck his middle finger up at her again.

The girl quickly turned back to the safety of her mum and dad.

"Will you stop doing that," Fanny said.

Hugh threw his head back and laughed, clutching his jiggling stomach.

"So mature," chastised Fanny.

Hugh wiped a tear from his eye. "What? That was funny —"

A green glow caught his eye, cutting him off. The glow came from his wrist and the third hand on his peculiar watch.

"Fuck."

A breeze cut across the swimming pool, the stifling heat replaced with a spine tingling cold. The swimmers in the pool started shivering and rubbing their bare arms. The puddle of sweat slopping about Hugh's nether regions felt like it turned to ice.

Fanny leaned forward in her chair. "Here we go. The show is about to begin."

Hugh swallowed. He didn't like how excited she sounded.

Right on cue, the folded-up plastic seats surrounding Hugh and Fanny flapped and rattled in a loud chorus of unorganised applause.

A scream of the *I'm terrified* variety came from the poolside below. A splash followed, then another, and another. Those stood at the side of the pool were falling into the water—lifeguards and all.

Hugh stood up.

"Shit. We need to get down there."

"But we will get a better view from up here." Fanny smiled, revealing a disgusting set of faded brown teeth which probably smelled like 150-year-old dog shit. Not for the first time, Hugh was glad he didn't have to endure the smell of the supernatural. He only had to endure Fanny's personality, which was more than enough.

Another scream came from the pool below. The water frothed and swirled like waves crashing against rocks. The scream had come from a lifeguard, his bald head disappearing under the churning water as his arms flapped wildly.

Some lifeguard he was.

Hugh sighed, what a way to spend his Saturday.

"Come on, let's get down there before someone drowns."

"Or, let's stay up here and watch them all drown," said Fanny, not moving.

For someone who liked to hang around the living, Fanny wasn't always keen on helping them survive. Apparently, she only stayed to help the lost souls move across the veil to the other side, not stop the useless living from bringing it on themselves.

"So bloody helpful," said Hugh, and he pushed off his cane toward the stairs, limping straight through Fanny. A tooth chattering chill flickered up his spine as he stepped through her and into the aisle of the stand.

Fanny hissed at him. It was rude to walk through a ghost after all.

"Get lost," said Hugh with a dismissive wave of his hand, "if you will not help then bugger off to where you belong."

He shouldn't have said that. The girl was very sensitive about moving across the veil and, truthfully; he needed her to help other lost souls pass across.

"I'm sorry," said Hugh, holding up his hands.

Fanny sat back and crossed her arms over her body. She stared ahead of her, her bottom lip poking out and blood dripped down her chin.

"Come on, I need you and you don't *really* want these people to die."

"One could not care less. They could keep me company and it would be better company than you."

More screams came from the pool, and the volume of the crashing water increased. Hugh turned away from his pissed off partner, almost grateful for the distraction.

Almost.

A turning, twisting, deadly circle of water was spinning at the centre of the pool, dragging the flapping swimmers towards it like fish being dragged in by a trawler's net.

Hugh limped at pace down the stairs towards the chaos.

Chaos. Apparently, this means complete disorder and confusion. An understatement then for what Hugh stepped into as he limped onto the tiled floor by the pool, which had turned into a sucking vortex of death.

Freezing cold water sloshed over the side and covered his shoes like he was aboard a pirate ship in a storm. Screams from swimmers filled his ears. Chlorine battled with the familiar metallic tang of the supernatural clawing the back of his throat.

He scanned the pool in search of whatever was causing the chaos. Bodies were everywhere. An old woman dressed in a tartan swimming costume was trying to drag what must have been her husband from the pool. The old boy was thrashing like a toddler having a tantrum, as the water grabbed at his legs.

A group of children were holding onto the swimming lane rope as it swung wildly like an octopus tentacle whilst their parents dove in from the side to save them.

The bald lifeguard who fell in whilst Hugh sat in the stands was still flapping his way towards the edge of the pool, as if he had only just learned how to swim. Every time the lifeguard looked like he was going to escape, the vortex of water pulled him back under.

Hugh stepped towards him and extended his cane for the man to grab hold of. Large beads of sweat dripped from Hugh's eyebrows and streaked across his face, blurring his vision. The pissing heat in this place was driving him nuts.

"Fanny, I need you!"

"One is here," said the girl, appearing by his side from thin air. Her voice was monotone, her expression blank, as if nothing was going on around her.

"Go find whatever is causing this, I need to stop some of these people from drowning."

"How is one going to find anything in amongst all this?"

Hugh gritted his teeth. "You're a fucking ghost. Surely you can find other ghosts, otherwise what's the point of you?"

He shouldn't have said that either.

Fanny's nostrils flared, and the gash on her head seemed to expand and contract.

"Sorry but—"

"Urrrrrgggggghhhh!"

A gargled cry for help interrupted Hugh's apology and he turned to see the lifeguard sinking under the water. His thrashing arms sent pool water splashing over the sides and onto Hugh's trousers. The whirlpool in the centre was just too strong, dragging him back like a huge, swirling magnet.

Hugh leaned further over the edge of the pool until the cane was almost in touching distance of the drowning man's arms.

"Grab on!" cried Hugh.

The man reached for the cane, but another wave of water engulfed him, dragging him under.

"Fanny, *please*. I need your help," said Hugh.

"Do you now?" said Fanny, not moving and tilting her head to the ceiling like an aloof Princess.

The lifeguard made another grab for the cane, this time getting a finger on it before the churning water dragged him back.

"Fanny, come on, I said sorry. You're not just a ghost you are a—"

"Detective?" she said, her eyes sliding to look at Hugh but her chin remaining tilted away.

"That's pushing it," said Hugh, grunting with the effort of trying not to fall in the pool and join the rest of the swimmers—the chlorine would ruin his suit after all.

Fanny pouted and crossed her arms.

"Alright, alright, you are a detective as well. One of the best partners I've ever worked with. Now can you please find whatever shit is doing this so we can stop them?"

The cane in Hugh's hand tugged him forward. He turned to help drag the lifeguard to the side of the pool. Except it wasn't a lifeguard holding the other end of the cane.

It was a young girl.

A young girl with grey dead looking skin.

A young girl with razor-sharp teeth in her grinning mouth.

Hugh pushed down the fourteen swear words on the tip of his tongue and squeezed tighter on the cane.

The girl slowly emerged from the water wearing a faded red and white striped swimsuit.

Her slicked back black hair revealed a large dent in her temple which had probably killed her.

Yet here she was, rising from the water like the child version of a kraken.

She snarled at Hugh and pulled harder on the cane.

He jolted forward and his arm felt like it had almost been pulled out of its socket.

"No!"

With whirling arms, he fell towards the pool and the snarling maw of the ghost.

Breaking the surface of the water with a thunderous splash, his mouth, nose, and ears filled as he disappeared under the surface.

"One has found the ghost", said Fanny, cheerfully from the side of the pool.

Hugh blinked; his vision blurred from the chemicals in the pool.

The soles of his bare feet felt cold against the tiled floor and the backside of his swimsuit felt crammed halfway up his arse.

Wait.

He blinked, clearing his vision, and found he was standing at the side of the pool again.

Only the chaos was gone.

The screams were still there, except they were the cries and calls of kids having fun. There was no churning whirlpool of death sucking swimmers under, only playful splashing. And best of all, there were no demon ghosts with half their heads caved in, emerging from the depths to drag Hugh under.

In fact, the whole inside of the Commonwealth Pool looked different—older, more familiar. Tattered peeling paintwork covered the walls whilst the tiles under his pretty pink painted toes looked a tired beige.

Wait...pretty pink toes?

Hugh looked down at his feet, only they weren't *his* feet. His toes were small and dainty—not gnarled and hairy. He admired them, drumming them against the tiled floor. It had been a while since he had even seen his toes. Normally, they were hidden by the vast mountain range that was his gut. His gut was gone, replaced with a small stomach wrapped in a red and white swimming costume.

Hugh didn't remember putting that on this morning. It was far too uncomfortable judging by how much of it his backside was chewing on.

He reached round and grabbed a handful of the costume and pulled it from his surprisingly small bum.

"Sarah, stop picking at your bum!"

Hugh turned towards the mocking voice. Stood next to him, with a wicked grin on his face, was a boy who must have been in his early teens. Greasy looking hair covered his head and his fringe hung so low it touched his spotty chin. A sea of oversized black clothes swathed his scrawny body.

Hugh didn't like teenage shits like this at the best of times, but right here, right now, he hated this boy with a visceral rage.

"Dirty bum! Dirty bum! Sarah's got a dirty bum!"

"Leave me alone Davie!" Hugh heard himself say in a light girlish whine.

"I will if you leave your dirty bum alone."

Hugh stomped his small, dainty feet on the tiles.

"I don't have a dirty bum!"

"Maybe you need to put your dirty bum back in the pool, clean it off," said Davie, his grin widening underneath his slimy black hair.

Hugh would not take this anymore. He turned away from Davie towards a group of women.

"Mum," moaned Hugh, "he said he's going to push me in again."

The closest of the group was a plump woman with black hair who wore an Adidas tracksuit with popping buttons up the side. Hugh hadn't seen one of those fashion disasters since he was twenty-five years younger and a good five stone lighter. The woman was gabbing away to another, who was wearing an equally garish tracksuit.

Boy, was Hugh glad he had dodged that fashion faux pas.

"Mum!" Hugh whined. Had he always sounded this much of a moan?

The woman turned, a mask of irritation on her tired face.

"What is it Sarah?"

"Davie said he was going to push me in the pool."

The woman tutted and said, "Davie Shaw, will you give it a rest with her."

Hugh turned towards Davie, looking forward to the seeing the shame on the boy's face. Maybe even some tears for getting into trouble.

Davie shrugged his shoulders as if he was being persecuted for a crime he never committed.

The woman turned back to her conversation, apparently satisfied she had dealt with the situation.

Hugh frowned. Was that *it*? Was that all the punishment Davie was going to get?

Not again.

Davie strode towards Hugh, a grin playing at the edge of his lips.

Brushing past Hugh, he leaned in and whispered, "Smelly bum, smelly bum, Sarah's got a smelly bum."

Hugh swung a small girlish fist at Davie's arm, but the boy was too quick, skipping out of her way, so she punched nothing but air.

The little shit turned and stuck his tongue back out at Hugh.

He wished he was his full size and he would crush the little turd's skull in his hands.

Ok maybe that was a little much.

But he *had* to get Davie back. Their Mum never knew how to punish them properly. Too busy chatting with her pals or busy with work. All she did was scream and shout at Davie—then go back to whatever she was doing.

That wasn't a real punishment.

No, what Davie needed was to be taught a lesson.

He needed to be pushed in the pool. With all his clothes on. *Yes*, that would teach him.

Davie had his back to Hugh now, his shoulders hunched over as he scuffed his black trainers in a puddle at the edge of the pool.

Hugh licked his lips, the familiar bristle of his moustache not there. He took a step towards Davie, placing one small foot in front of the other as he moved towards his prey.

Davie's head was down, as always. He was so miserable, always had been since Dad left. No wonder he had no pals.

Hugh was almost within touching distance now. He held his breath and raised his hands. This was it—payback.

He jumped forward just as Davie turned on his feet.

Hugh only caught the edge of the boy's shirt and he stumbled forward towards the pool.

Trying to plant his feet to stop himself from falling, Hugh's left foot landed in the puddle Davie had been splashing in.

He felt his foot slip from underneath him. The tile floor came at him far too fast.

He raised his hands, but he was too late.

The impact of the tile against his soft head caused the lights in the pool's ceiling to shudder and spin. Inside his head, the blow sounded like a hammer being taken to an egg.

Then there was nothing but cold as the pool swallowed up his limp body.

"Sarah!" came a muffled cry, "somebody get her out!"

But Hugh was under the water, watching the lights and shadows flicker above.

He would try to kick his legs to the surface if he could, but for some reason, these new skinny little legs were even heavier than the fat pair he was used to.

The shadows moving above the surface of the water blurred.

He could hear a shout, "I told you not to push her again! Look what you've done, you stupid boy—"

Hugh wanted to cry back. It hadn't been Davie's fault.

It was just a silly mistake.

But a gargle of water filled his throat.

Just a silly mistake.

His eyes slowly closed, fading out the dark shadows above...

...Hugh coughed.

Spluttered.

Then rolled onto his side and spat out a mouthful of chlorine tasting water.

"Delightful," said a voice above him.

He groaned and rolled onto his back. Fanny appeared above him, along with the metallic taste at the back of his throat. She showed her rotting teeth in a bemused smile.

Hugh was almost relieved to see her.

There was a puddle in Hugh's arse again, only it wasn't sweat. It was pool water, and he was soaked in it, his suit ruined.

"Fucking hell, what was that all about? I was a little girl —"

Hugh grabbed at his stomach through his sodden shirt and gave it a shake, relieved to feel its familiar weight in his hands.

"I think you made a new friend," said Fanny.

"I think I *was* the new friend."

Fanny pursed her lips and scratched at her scab.

"Is everyone ok?" asked Hugh.

"The screaming's stopped, if that is what you are asking? Your new friend stopped the show once she pulled you under. Who was she?"

"Sarah Shaw and apparently we need to find her mum. Right after I've changed my clothes and—"

"Let me guess. Had a stiff drink?"

"Good guess, Detective Archibald."

A month later, Detective Hugh McRath was poolside and sweating again. Thankfully, the circumstances were slightly different.

He was still sitting in the stands of the Royal Commonwealth Pool, but the cries and shouts coming from the swimmers were from a place of fun rather than terrifying fear. There was still a metallic tang in the air, which told him his partner Fanny wasn't far away, but thankfully, no ghosts were trying to pull him under the water and back in time.

Hugh also had company, and not of the supernatural variety.

Sat next to him in the stands was Mrs Shaw. The woman's black hair had sprouted a patch of grey at the crown since Hugh saw her standing at the side of the pool in her Adidas tracksuit.

Thankfully, the tracksuit was gone, but her clothes were no less depressing to Hugh. She had on a tired brown cardigan worn out at the sleeves, with a pair of black joggers covered in suspicious stains and scuffed white trainers.

The passage of time, and by the looks of her yellow stained fingers, a serious smoking habit, had done its damage to her face. Deep lines spread across the puffy black bags under her eyes and her skin hung loose from her gaunt cheekbones. She sat picking at a scab on her thumb whilst her right leg bounced constantly.

Tracking down Mrs Shaw hadn't been too difficult. Convincing her to come back to the scene of her daughter's death had been. In the end Hugh had to lie and tell her there had been some items found that may have belonged to her. A ridiculous reason, but Hugh knew she would show up because her daughter Sarah had known her mother was ready.

The dead just know. And they let Hugh know so he could help.

Sarah had picked the 25th anniversary of her death to contact her mother. It was just a shame she had used haunting the swimming pool as a way of communicating. Life would have been a lot easier for Hugh if she could just use email.

"Christ, this place makes me need a fag," said Mrs Shaw.

"When was the last time you visited?"

Mrs Shaw looked down at her finger as she picked away a part of her skin.

"July 22nd, 1996."

Hugh nodded. "The day Sarah died."

Mrs Shaw said nothing and instead rubbed at the blood seeping from where she had picked away the skin.

"What can you tell me about that day?" prodded Hugh.

A raspy sigh left Mrs Shaw's lungs.

"We were there for her swimming lessons. She wasn't the strongest swimmer my Sarah, so we decided some lessons during the summer would help. God, she had moaned that morning about going. I had spent half the morning screaming and shouting at her to get ready. If I had just let her miss—"

The words caught in her throat and she went back to picking at the scab on her finger.

Hugh let the silence between them sit for a moment as he gazed down at the pool. Two boys were wrestling and mucking about at the side, trying to throw each other in. A sharp whistle rang from the opposite end of the pool. It was the bald lifeguard Hugh had been trying to fish from the pool a month ago before Sarah had emerged and dragged Hugh under.

The two boys stopped wrestling at the sound of the whistle and stood, heads bowed like good, repentant children.

When the lifeguard turned away from them, one of the boys stuck the v's up at him before pushing his friend into the pool.

Everything was back to normal.

According to Edinburgh Council, a fault with the filtration system had caused the disaster, which almost drowned a swimming pool full of swimmers. Not the spirit of a girl who died twenty-five years ago trying to pass on a message to her mum. To be fair, the first explanation was probably easier for the general public to swallow.

"Your son Davie," said Hugh, breaking the silence.

Mrs Shaw's body stiffened next to Hugh.

"Yeah, what of him?"

"He was here on the day your daughter died?"

Mrs Shaw stopped picking at the scab on her finger.

"Of course he was. It's that little shit's fault she is gone. Pushed her in. But she was only little—"

The words caught in her throat again and she lifted her finger to her mouth, chewing at the scab.

"Did you see him push her?" asked Hugh.

Mrs Shaw removed her finger from her mouth and frowned at Hugh.

"What sort of question is that? Of course it was him. Always causing trouble that one. Trying to wind his sister up. Nipping at her, teasing her and never leaving her alone. Bane of my *bloody* existence."

So, she hadn't seen anything, thought Hugh.

"And how is he now?"

"How the hell would I know," Mrs Shaw said, her voice spiced with bitterness, "we had a falling out a long time ago. The boy doesn't even send his own mother a birthday card these days. That's the type of son I got given."

Hugh thought of the last time his daughter sent him a card. Three years ago? Or was it five? Time just melted away at his age. He couldn't blame her though. That had been all his fault.

"Your watch is broken," Mrs Shaw said, pulling him from that painful thought.

Hugh blinked and glanced down at his peculiar watch. The long hand was pointing to his right whilst the middle hand spun constantly. Thankfully, there was no green glow coming from the smallest hand, but the familiar creep of cold worked its way up his spine and the metallic taste grew stronger in his mouth.

He glanced to his right to find two bodies sat next to him, their colours washed out like they were made from tracing paper. Two seats along sat Sarah Shaw—still dressed in her wet, red and white striped swimsuit. The dent, still visible beneath her slicked back hair, gave her forehead an unnatural shape. Water dripped from her but left no traces on the ground at her bare feet. Her legs hung over the edge of her seat and she swung them back and forth playfully.

Hugh recognised the pink on her toes even though it had lost some of its vibrancy. She smiled at him, revealing those sharp fangs which had snarled as she emerged from the pool a month ago.

"You are sweating again," said the girl closer to Hugh. It was Fanny, in her usual black dress, the wound in her head still dripping.

The girls held hands, both staring at Hugh and smiling expectantly.

Two dead girls, killed through fatal head injuries, sitting smiling at him in their ghostly forms. It was at times like this Hugh was reminded why he drank so much.

Nonetheless, Hugh smiled back at them both.

"Is our new friend ready to leave?" he asked Fanny.

His partner nodded in response.

"Who are you talking to?" said Mrs Shaw, irritation slipping into her tone, "and why am I here? Do you think I want to go through this all again? I've got better things to do with my Saturday you know."

Hugh turned in his seat, trying to ignore the sweat trickling down his forehead. Mrs Shaw stared at him, tired eyes glaring, her mouth a thin line.

Hugh suddenly felt a wave of exhaustion hit him. It was always tricky, this stage of the process. How do you explain to someone what they have believed for so long is untrue? That they have been punishing themselves and others for something which wasn't their fault. The hatred and anger helping them cope with the grief. But ultimately, this would wear them down and kill them in the end. Eating them from the inside out like a cancerous tumour.

It was almost easier to explain he was sitting next to two ghosts.

At least then he would just be labelled as insane. He was used to that.

"Go on, tell her. Sarah says she is ready," said Fanny, reassuringly.

Hugh glanced to his right and both the girls smiled and nodded in unison. Which would have been comforting if it wasn't so fucking creepy.

He turned to face Mrs Shaw. "I know at the time of Sarah's death you think you saw Davie pushing his sister, which caused her to slip and bang her head."

Her gaze moved to the scab on her hand, unable to meet Hugh's. He gripped the cane by his side tighter. She knows, thought Hugh.

"You did see him push her, Mrs Shaw?"

She shook her head and pulled her cardigan tight around her.

"Of course I bloody did. It was his fault—," but she couldn't finish that sentence.

"You don't know that for certain, do you?" said Hugh, keeping his voice soft.

Sarah's mother didn't respond.

"You don't know, as you had your back to your daughter when she fell in, as you were talking to your friends."

Mrs Shaw covered her eyes with her hands.

"Stop—"

"It's ok. I know you didn't see her fall and slip by herself."

Mrs Shaw's shoulders were shaking now. Hugh wanted to stop the pain for her, but he knew if Sarah was going to allow herself to be taken across the veil to the dead, then he had to pass on one more message to her grieving Mother.

"It wasn't Davie's fault. It was just an unfortunate accident. A silly mistake."

A sob escaped Mrs Shaw's throat.

"You don't need to blame him or anyone else anymore," said Hugh, placing his hand on her shoulder and giving it a reassuring squeeze.

Her body shuddered. The years of anger and guilt shaking themselves out of her.

"She is ready now," said Fanny, "I will take her across the veil."

Hugh looked towards the two girls.

"Maybe you should stay with her on the other side?" whispered Hugh. He didn't mean that, he would miss the girl if she did, but then he also wanted her to get some rest.

Fanny shook her head. "How would one scare you if one was across the veil?"

Hugh smiled. "See you soon then, partner."

Fanny beamed, a gristly disgusting yet somehow beautiful smile, before turning to Sarah and nodding reassuringly at the little girl.

Sarah waved at Hugh then slowly, like a wisp of smoke being blown away by an invisible wind, the girls faded, leaving Hugh and Mrs Shaw sat in the stands alone.

Mrs Shaw had stopped crying, but her head remained bowed, and Hugh still had a comforting hand on her shoulder. The gold face of his peculiar watch poked out from under the sleeve of his shirt. If this had been a normal watch, all the hands would have been facing to noon.

Hugh started to sweat again, the clawing heat causing beads to run down his back and gather in the crack of his arse. The icy chill in the air had gone, as was the metallic taste in his mouth. He was in need of a stiff drink.

Everything was back to normal. For now.

Except it wasn't for Mrs Shaw.

So, Hugh sat there in comfortable silence for a long time with the grieving woman and watched the swimmers splash and play in the pool. Whilst they sat, he thought about the passing of time, forgiveness, and family grievances.

Rewriting the Past

The bell chimed as Detective Hugh McRath limped into the second-hand bookstore.

The entrance to the store was a tunnel of book-lined shelves which pressed down on Hugh as soon as he walked inside. His girth and the tight space meant his good suit jacket rubbed against all the filthy used books. He wrinkled his large purple nose, his moustache twitching at the dust and the musty old feet smell. The three-piece suit he was wearing would get dry cleaned or burned tomorrow, that was for sure.

Why did the dead always interrupt his strolls around Edinburgh by dragging him to stinking places like this?

Hugh hadn't made it far in today's leisurely walk around the Old Town (although he rarely did, the pain in his hip and the call to go to the pub were always too strong). But today, only a few hundred yards from his flat, his watch started to complain, dragging him huffing and moaning down to the Grassmarket. He had the choice to ignore the watch, of course, but if he did, the thing would bleat and grumble all day. As would his conscience.

On his journey, he passed at least ten perfectly acceptable pubs he could drink the rest of the day away in before being stopped in front of this bookstore. The watch, which had turned his mood foul (well, fouler), was no regular watch and its spinning hands told Hugh all pretence of a pleasant day had been thrown out of the window. His watch told him this, as did the metallic taste of the dead, which appeared in the back of his throat as soon as he had stepped into the stale smelling store.

The watch and the taste were signs the dead were present and were normally accompanied by—

"Look at all these books, marvellous," whispered a girl's voice in his ear.

"Shit!" Hugh staggered away from the voice, colliding with a shelf of books, and sending a couple of thick tombs tumbling to the ground. Dust particles flew up all around him, catching in Hugh's nose. He pushed himself back off the shelf with his cane, his other hand reaching for the pocket square in the front of his suit, but he didn't make it to his nose in time and let out a roaring sneeze. The books surrounding Hugh quickly swallowed up the spray of snot floating with the dust particles. He dreaded to think how many more sneezes those same brown tinged books had swallowed in the past.

"Bless you," said the girl.

Hugh wiped his nose and thick grey moustache with the pocket square and looked towards the girl without thanking her for her blessings.

Stood against the backdrop of mismatched book spines was Fanny Archibald, dressed as always in a black dress which covered every inch of her except her neck and head. A constant stream of fresh blood flowed from a wound on her forehead and covered her face. The wound seemed to quiver and pulse as if there were insects crawling inside the girl's skull. No doubt there were. The 15-year-old was murdered back in 1865 by someone who had been particularly useful with a butcher's blade. Who the chef was and why they took a particular interest in Fanny's skull, Hugh had yet to find out.

Unfortunately, the tight lip didn't extend to her thoughts on how he should handle the dead. Hugh liked to ignore her thoughts as much as possible and remind the girl her role was to help the dead back across the veil, the place where the dead should reside—not here amongst the living, ruining Hugh's day.

"Do you have to creep up on me like that?" said Hugh, "it's bad enough your lot make me come in a place like this. Now you are trying to make me touch these disgusting books."

Fanny smiled and two small black spiders crawled out of her mouth, down her chin and disappeared into the neck of her dress. Hugh chewed the inside of his mouth. No matter how much time he spent in the girl's company, he would never get used to the sight of things crawling about her face.

"Only you would not like books. You are such a philistine," she said.

"I never said I didn't like books. I just don't like musty old books. They remind me too much of the dead and I am fucking sick of dead things."

"Charming," said Fanny, turning her back on Hugh and perusing the shelves behind her. The back of her head was a greasy mess of hair and looked like it would take some industrial strength bleach to get it looking close to clean again.

Hugh frowned and shifted his gaze back into the tunnel entrance of the bookstore. The corridor of books turned sharply left about ten yards in front of Hugh, making it impossible to see who or what was waiting for him further into the shop. Hugh hated the doubt of not knowing what lay ahead of him.

"So, why are we here?" he said.

"How should I know?" Fanny said.

"Come on, Fanny—"

"Detective Archibald."

Despite her age and her complete lack of experience, Fanny still liked to think she was a detective just because she helped Hugh out.

"I keep tellin' you. Your name is Fanny, not Detective Archibald. You've not put the hours in to call yourself a detective. Come back to me when you've put thirty years of graft in."

Fanny looked over her shoulder, her neck turning more than Hugh was comfortable watching. She arched an eyebrow at him and the wound on her head expanded, another trickle of blood dribbled down her face.

"May I remind you, *detective*," she said, "I have been dead since 1865. If we are measuring in years, I outrank you. And, despite my age, I still look younger than you."

A little harsh from the dead girl with spiders crawling over her face. She turned her head back to the bookshelves.

"Ok, *Detective* Archibald," grumbled Hugh, "why are we here? You usually have an inkling of these things, seen as you are…well…dead."

Fanny didn't respond as she stared at the cover of a book which had a bare-chested man with an unrealistically chiselled jaw on the front.

"Oh, my—"

"Fanny. Eyes off the nipples. A detective always maintains focus. Why are we here?"

Fanny didn't take her eyes off the book and the nipples of the novels love interest.

"I don't know why you are here, but I know why I am now," she said, absentmindedly reaching up and stroking the cover. Her fingertips passed through the book as they trailed their way down the pouting models' rock-hard abs.

"Excellent. Thanks for your input, detective, it was about as useful as a chocolate teapot," said Hugh.

He guessed he would just have to find out for himself. Placing the snot smeared pocket square back into his front pocket, he straightened out his coat, adjusted the bowler hat on his head and brushed down whatever clung to him from this wretched place. Hugh limped further into the store, flicking the two books he had knocked off their shelf out of his way with his cane.

Despite her fascination with the disturbingly attractive muscled man on the front of the book, Hugh could feel Fanny following him. The hairs on the back of his neck stood to attention as she crept behind him. She always followed—the nosy cow. But then he wasn't sure what he would do if she didn't; it's not like he could accompany the dead across the veil. Well, he could, but then it would be his turn to join them. No, Hugh's job was to figure out what the dead wanted resolved, not hold their hand on the way back across the veil.

The floorboards creaked under his weight and the musty smell thickened as he walked further into the cramped bookstore.

"Hurry up *laddie,* and get this rung up," a rough accent called from deeper in the store. It was a man's voice, his booming demand meeting Hugh's ears as he rounded the corner into another tunnel of books.

"S-s-sorry I don't know what is wrong with the till," stuttered another man's response.

"Just get a bloody move on!"

The tunnel in front of Hugh opened out into a wider but no less cramped space. There were books piled in tottering towers in every corner. A collection of tattered paperbacks seemed to have devoured a table in the centre of the space. Shunted in the room's corner, behind a protective wall of books, was a tired-looking desk on which sat more books and an ancient looking till. Behind the desk, a man in a ragged cardigan frantically tapped at the till. He looked like he would happily disappear under the desk until all customers in the shop left him alone to his books.

Towering over him from the other side was a thick man dressed in a tweed suit, his red hair sprinkled with grey. In his hand he held a worn hardback.

"Come on. Come on. Get a move on," the man waved his hands as he spoke, swinging the hardback like a baseball bat reminding Hugh of Robert DeNiro in *The Untouchables,* dealing with incompetence in his crew. The gentle and apparently inept bookseller flinched with every wave of the hardback in Bobby DeNiro's hand.

Now Hugh didn't like incompetence either. Christ knows, he had been used to it when he worked in the police and he had handed out countless bollockings because of it. But what he hated more than anything in the world was bullies. He had done ever since he was a child at school, facing up to the bullies who used to pick on the runt of the litter in class. Most of the time the bullies were the teachers, but Hugh had no problem standing up to them either and certainly would have no issue standing up to the man waving the book at the bookseller—in fact, he was in the mood for an argument.

"Is there a problem here?" he asked.

The man holding the book stopped swinging the weapon and turned to glare at Hugh, his cheeks tinged red and thick eyebrows knitted in a frown.

"That's none of your business pal," he said, spittle flying from his mouth as he spoke.

The man behind the desk looked towards Hugh, his wide-eyed gaze pleading for help.

"Oh, I don't know about that," said Hugh, limping further into the space towards the desk.

"Are you the owner of this establishment?" demanded the red-haired man. It seemed to Hugh the man was used to making demands.

Hugh snorted. "God no. Not much of a reader me, especially not books touched by too many grubby hands."

"Philistine," whispered Fanny in his ear. Hugh ignored her.

"Then you cannae help and you can mind your business," said the red-haired man, turning away from Hugh towards the desk.

The book seller flinched, his wide eyes on the red-haired man as he spoke, "Mr Martty—"

"Martin. It's Mr Charles Martin, you useless prick."

"S-s-sorry, yes Mr Martin. Mr Martin here has been trying to find this book everywhere and I have finally secured him a copy, but my till seems to have stopped working."

The bookseller was trying to drag Hugh into the conversation, no doubt hoping the extra eyewitness in the room would protect him from a beating.

He needn't have worried; Hugh was fully engaged now. There was a reason his watch called him to *this* bookstore, after all.

"Your till has stopped working? How strange."

"Oooooooooooo spooky!" cried Fanny, in a deep, chilling voice only Hugh could hear.

He crushed the handle of his cane but ignored her again.

Charles turned to Hugh. "Yes, very strange. Still none of your business."

As he spoke, a blob of spittle at the side of his mouth bobbed up and down. Hugh wondered how the same blob would look smeared over his knuckles after he cracked this ejit in the face.

Hugh hobbled next to the desk, leaning on his cane. Up close, the desk was even more chaotic. Reams of paper and dusty looking books with frayed edges covered every inch of its surface. Sprinkled over the top were several biro pens, each of them in differing chewed states. Three half-drunk cups of tea sat festering in stained mugs.

"This is a rather disorganised fellow, is he not?" Fanny said, stating the obvious as always. She circled the desk, the two other men in the room none the wiser to her presence.

Only Hugh had that *pleasure*. Lucky him.

Hugh ignored her comment. "What is the name of the book?" he asked Charles.

Charles took a step towards Hugh, puffing his chest out. He was close enough now for Hugh to see the maze of veins on the end of the man's nose. He smelled of drink—possibly last nights but you never knew with some people. There were plenty out there who loved to pour whisky over their cornflakes in the morning.

Some people. Who was he kidding? He wished he had done the same this morning—again.

Hugh swallowed, the stale smell of alcohol coming from Charles not putting him off the thought of drink, if anything it made him thirstier.

"Did you not hear me? It is none of your business," said Charles, the sneer on his face revealing yellow stained teeth.

Hugh gripped his cane tighter. If the man was ready for a fight, then Hugh would give him one, but first he would try the civilised route.

"Listen here, you big prick," he said, "I'm a detective, I came here as part of my investigations and find you abusing this man."

Technically, this wasn't a lie. He was a detective, just of the supernatural.

He continued making his civilised points. "If you don't take your ugly mug a step back, then I'll have you dragged away and thrown in a cell."

"Can you have him thrown in a cell? I thought you were not a *real* detective anymore," asked Fanny, appearing behind Charles' shoulder.

Hugh ignored the girl's factual statement.

Charles eyed him up and down, the sneer not leaving his face. "You. A detective? Since when do the police dress like Poirot?"

"Who is Poirot?" asked Fanny.

"Mind your business," growled Hugh at Fanny.

"No detective," said Charles, leaning in so close his nose was almost touching Hugh's, "I said you should mind yours."

"Now, now. Please, we cannot have fighting in the shop. Think of the mess you would make," said the bookseller, his voice a high-pitched squeak. He banged on the till and it sprung open, the change inside rattling.

"Ah, there we go! See. No need to fight. That will be four —"

A hard-looking object flew across Hugh's vision so fast a breeze brushed his face. He flinched, breaking his staring match with Charles. A loud crunching sound filled the room, followed by a thud.

Hugh looked behind the desk. Lying on his back was the bookseller. He was out cold, his nose twisted in an unnatural shape, blood streaming down his lips and chin. A large book lay open by his head.

"Why did you do that? I needed him," said Charles, his voice incredulous.

Hugh looked up at the man, who was staring at him in disbelief.

"What are talking about? That was you."

Charles raised the book in his hand and pointed it towards Hugh. "Now listen here. I did nothing of the sort. You are not framing me. I saw the book fly through the air. It had to be you."

"Impossible," said Hugh.

Impossible. A word the dead seemed to see as a challenge whenever Hugh made the mistake of uttering it.

"Detective, I think we may have found the reason we are here," said Fanny, a touch of glee in the girl's voice. Hugh's stomach flipped; a joyful Fanny was never a good sign.

A hard object thumped into Hugh's elbow, a shooting pain travelling down his arm, forcing him to drop his cane, which clattered to the floor.

"You bastard," said Hugh, clutching his elbow.

"Who threw that?!" said Charles.

Hugh looked at the book at his feet. The cover read *The Strange Case of Dr Jekyll and Mr Hyde.*

Bloody ghosts.

"Are you trying to set me up?" shouted Charles.

Hugh looked at the man's face, twisted with rage.

He took a step towards Hugh. "Because let me tell you, it won't work."

"Oh, shut up, you twat. Why would I want someone to set you up by throwing books at me?"

Charles swung the book he held in his hand in front of Hugh's face. "Because you want what's in here."

"What are you talking about? I have never seen that book before in my life."

"Liar. It's mine, you'll need to pry the book out of my dead hands." The man pounded the book against his chest with each sentence like a gorilla protecting its territory in the jungle.

Hugh frowned. "Listen, I don't know what you are banging—"

But Hugh didn't have time to answer as another book cracked him across the side of his head, sending his bowler hat to the floor. He let out a grunt and a shower of white light flashed behind his eyes.

"I would duck if I were you," said Fanny.

Her timing and help were impeccable, as always.

Another book struck him in the back, followed by a sharp-edged hardback in his bad hip almost sending him to the floor.

Then the books were showering down on him like giant hailstones.

"What's going on!" cried Charles, the anger and certainty stripped away from his voice, and replaced with fear.

The dead will do that to a man.

Hugh raised his arms to cover his head as paper and books flew all around him, sounding like a flock of pigeons.

Fanny cackled, her laugh cutting through the noise. She always got excited when the dead paid a visit. The innocent young girl, taken over by the excitement of her friends from across the veil coming to play.

The hard edges of the books kept finding their targets like the accurate blows of a professional boxer.

Chest. Back. Stomach. Knee. Hip. Arse.

Calling the last shot accurate was unfair. Hugh's arse was a large target.

The constant blows threatened to send him to the ground. But if he went down, he knew he would never get back up.

He staggered towards the desk the bookseller had stood behind. Books slammed into him as he rolled over the top with all the grace of a pig rolling in its own shit. The till slid off the desk with him, scattering mainly coins across the floor. Hugh landed with a jarring thud on his arse before turning and crawling under the desk. He felt like he was in an air raid shelter as more books thudded against the wood over his head.

Peering out from under his shelter, he found Charles through the swirling mass of books. The man cowered against the shelves as book after book slammed into him. Yet he didn't go down or let go of the book he had been swinging at Hugh, clutching it to his chest like a child holding his favourite comfort blanket.

Through the blur of paper and pain, Hugh noticed the blows attacking Charles were targeting his arms and hands, as if trying to prize the book from him.

"Get under here!" shouted Hugh over the storm of books.

"No thanks, this is fun!" called Fanny back.

"I wasn't talking to you," said Hugh. The girl grinned at him, her dead eyes looking almost alive as books whipped around and through her. It was at times like this Hugh wondered if she was *actually* any help at all.

He turned his attention back to the other man being attacked.

"Mr Martin, over here!"

But the man wasn't listening, screaming, and yelling, whilst swiping wildly at the attacking books.

A particularly accurate shot from a thin hardback caught Charles in the fingers. He yelped and dropped the prized possession he had been swinging in Hugh's face only moments ago.

"No!" he shouted and dove after the book, landing on top of it and pressing himself to the floor.

Hugh shook his head in disbelief. What was it about that book that was so special?

The storm of paper and jagged edges (or whatever directed them) took advantage of Charles' stupidity and rained down on him.

Thump. Thump. Thump.

Blow after blow cracked off his body.

One blow caught Charles behind the ear and he let out a groan. For a moment, Hugh thought the man might have joined the bookseller in the land of nod; instead he rolled his head to the side and looked directly into Hugh's eyes.

Hugh lifted a hand and beckoned the other man towards the desk he cowered under. Charles nodded and started to crawl towards Hugh. There was blood seeping out of his knuckles where the flying books had targeted him, but his hands still gripped to the apparently precious cargo.

"Drop the book," shouted Hugh.

Charles shook his head, his look defiant.

Hugh ground his teeth. Why was the man being such a fool? It wasn't like he wanted the book. Whatever was causing the storm was going to kill him, and he was too stubborn to give up what they wanted.

They wanted.

Something clicked in Hugh's mind.

Not they. Who?

In the chaos of the storm, he had forgotten why he was here.

He looked towards Fanny, who was now spinning on the spot, her arms outstretched, head tilted towards the ceiling, seemingly enjoying every moment of the storm.

"Fanny!" cried Hugh.

She lowered her head and looked at him, a wicked grin on her face.

Hugh didn't smile back. "Can you get whoever is doing this to come out?"

"But they might stop."

"That's kind of the point."

Her grin faded into a frown. "But they might be having fun."

"No. You are having fun," said Hugh, leaning forward and pointing a finger at the dead girl, "whoever is stuck on this side of the veil is suffering."

A bang over Hugh's head made him flitch and cower back under the table. A doorstop-sized book fell over the edge of the desk and landed on the floor next to Hugh. Hugh couldn't imagine why anyone would read a book that long. Being cracked over the skull would be a better use of paper.

The book wobbled and shook as if it was about to take off again. Hugh lunged forward and dragged the doorstop under the desk beside him. Christ, it was heavy. What was the author thinking writing a book this long? Who had the time and patience for that?

Hugh looked back out from under his shelter. Charles was no longer crawling towards Hugh, instead curled up in the fetal position as the books rained down on him.

Hugh leaned forward again, careful not to stick his head out from under the desk for fear of a book taking out his teeth. "Come on Fanny, before anyone gets hurt."

Fanny pouted and balled up her fists before whispering, "Hello, is anybody there?"

"What are you doing?" said Hugh.

"What does it sound like? One is trying to get whoever is putting on the show to come out."

"What just by whispering to the room?"

Fanny shrugged. "How else would I do it?"

Hugh pursed his lips. He had no idea.

"Carry on."

"Hello, is anybody there? Come out, come out wherever you are," she said, putting her hands on either side of her mouth.

Hugh shook his head. Ghosts were bloody ridiculous. Here he was, cowering for his life under a desk whilst the ghost who was trying to take his head off was playing hide and seek.

"I know you are out there ghost. Do not worry, one is not trying to harm you," called Fanny, her voice still a childish whisper.

Hugh folded his arms, taking breaths so deep and heavy that his moustache bristled. The stench of the old book filling his nose did nothing to help control his anger. This ghost better make an appearance soon or so help him.

"I say ghost, I say ghost, where are you?" said Fanny as she strolled amongst the chaos.

A book flew through her and cracked Charles in the back. The man barely moved in response. He looked as out cold as the bookseller. The book he had been holding spilled from his hands.

Fanny didn't even look in the man's direction as she stepped through him and continued to call out for the ghost in her gentle tone.

Hugh could hear his own teeth grinding in his skull at the girl's complete lack of urgency.

"Come on now ghost, out you come. I only want to play. I promise the mean nasty men will behave."

Another torrent of thuds landed on the table, shaking the wood above Hugh. He pressed his palms against the wood on either side of him just in case the table collapsed.

Right. Fuck this.

That was enough from this arsehole of a ghost.

He lunged towards the opening under the table but smacked his head off the wood.

"Ah ya bastard—" he said and reached for the now throbbing pain in his forehead. It felt like he had caved half his skull in.

Fanny hadn't noticed and was still muttering to the room. "I know he looks like a fat, ugly pig of a man with a terrible temper, and, well, he is all of those things, but I will help you."

Hugh thumped his fist against the inside of the desk. He had a terrible temper, did he? Well, she had seen nothing yet.

With the pumping adrenaline pushing the pain in his head from his mind, he placed his hands above him on the underside of the desk and began to push. The desk was built of thick wood, but Hugh's rage was made of thicker stuff and he lifted until he could get his two feet under himself.

Ignoring the savage pain in his hip, Hugh let out a roar and pushed the desk up and away from himself.

The desk crashed behind him and he rose out from underneath, back amongst the eye of the storm.

"That. Is. Enough! Whoever is doing this better show themselves right now!"

"Well, that was a touch dramatic," said Fanny.

Hugh turned to roar abuse at the girl but froze as all the surrounding books stopped moving. The paper stopped flapping. Everything just hovered for a second, then— dropped—crashing to the ground in one loud clap, sending a cloud of dust towards Hugh.

He tried to shield his face but was too late. Dust scratched at his eyes, immediately blinding him. A mouthful more caught at the back of his throat and he coughed and spluttered away the rank, mouldy taste.

Blinking away tears, he reached for his pocket square but remembered he had covered it in snot earlier. Instead, Hugh rubbed at his eyes and waited for the burning to stop. Bloody ghosts always dragging him to places that were covered in dust.

As he rubbed his eyes, he realised the surrounding room was silent.

Deathly silent. The hairs on the back of his neck prickled.

He blinked open his eyes and turned back to face the room.

The room looked like the wreckage after a hurricane. Books lay scattered everywhere, like rubble. He could make out the two humps of Charles Martin and the bookseller under the piles of books and paper, neither of them moving. Hugh couldn't decide if the room looked any less clean or dirty compared to how it looked when he first walked in.

Standing in amongst the wreckage was Fanny, still grinning as she rocked back and forth on the balls of her feet. And next to her, stooped over and leaning on a cane, was an old woman dressed like Fanny with her grey hair scraped back off her face. The old woman may have dressed from the same era as Fanny, but she was missing the youth and the gore.

But she was very much dead. The eyes gave her away, the blank stare cutting through him from under her drooping eyelids. That and the dozens of spiders crawling across her face.

"My name is Lady Campbell. I believe you were looking for me," she said, her voice a croak.

In her hand, she held the book Charles Martin had been trying so hard to protect.

Detective Hugh McRath sat on a pile of books opposite the dead woman.

Hugh had quickly found a place to plonk his backside after Lady Campbell had introduced herself. The effort of crawling about the floor and throwing the desk over his head had caught up on him. He knew the old woman sat opposite him would be exhausted as well. The effort of what she had just done wasn't easy for someone like her on this side of the veil. She sat perched on the end of the table, which had been covered in books before she had thrown them across the room. Well, she wasn't sitting on the table, more floating just above it.

Fanny was pacing as usual. The girl never seemed to stand still, like she had ants in her pants. Hugh supposed she probably *did* have ants in her pants.

There were no wounds on Lady Campbell's body judging by what Hugh could see, and the dead tended not to be subtle when it came to showing off the reason they were no longer among the living. Hugh had seen more blood and guts from ghosts than he had seen in all his time on the police force.

He supposed the woman died of old age, which made her appearance on this side of the veil even more intriguing. Those who had their life cut short tended to be angry enough to endure the pain of crossing back through the veil to the land of the living. Lady Campbell looked like someone who had lived a long and privileged life, although not necessarily a happy one, judging by the lack of cheer on her face.

"So, what is this all about?" said Hugh, nodding towards the surrounding bombsite.

She frowned, a couple of spiders crawled across her chin, down her turkey neck and disappearing into her dress.

Hugh swallowed down his disgust, the thick metallic taste of the dead stronger than ever in his mouth.

"It is Lady Campbell, I was not born into a family with history as rich as mine to not be addressed by my proper name," said the old woman, each syllable given an extra emphasis in her plummy posh accent.

Hugh shifted in his seat, the corner of a book digging into his backside. It was true; she didn't look like the kind of woman who was used to being talked down to by the likes of him and he really wasn't in the mood to have more hardbacks launched at his head. But god did her arrogance make him want to tell the wrinkly old bawbag to go fuck herself.

"Apologies, Lady Campbell. To what do we owe the pleasure of your presence on this side of the veil?"

You spooky fucking bitch.

"That is more like it," she said, meeting Hugh's gaze. Hugh could only look into those dull, dead eyes for a moment before he averted his gaze. The weight of what the dead could see always pushed a melancholy sadness on him he could never hold for too long.

"I am cleaning up a mess," she said.

"It looks to me like you are the one who made the mess," said Hugh, waving his hand toward the destroyed bookshop.

Lady Campbell shrugged. "Well, in my current condition, it is very difficult to exert my influence over a man like Charles."

"Given you are dead, your current condition certainly would make that difficult."

"Quite."

"And what kind of influence do you want to exert over Charles? Apart from smashing his skull in with the spine of a novel. Is it something to do with the book you hold in your hands?"

"None of those things is any of your business."

"I am not so sure, Lady Campbell. You have just knocked one man unconscious, and almost destroyed this man's business." Hugh pointed to the second lump on the floor, which was the bookseller.

Lady Campbell did not respond, staring off into the distance in stubborn silence.

Hugh had to get her talking, otherwise he wouldn't be able to help the old hag. Christ, he felt more like a psychiatrist than a detective these days. Where was his therapist for dealing with all this shit?

He tried a softer tactic. "I deal with the dead and you, I am afraid, are very much dead."

Ok maybe not soft. Hugh didn't really know how to do soft. But at least he was honest, and Lady Campbell didn't look like she suffered fools.

The edge of her lips curled in a smile—a spider took the opportunity to crawl out of her mouth and disappear up her nose.

"I can help you know," continued Hugh, his tone soft, "I want to. Tell me what is wrong, Lady Campbell. I know you must be tired coming across the veil and creating all of this mess."

Lady Campbell sighed, her stiff posture deflating momentarily. She shook her head. "What is the world coming to when I have to discuss family issues with a common detective. Thank goodness I died when I did. I am clearly not built for this modern world."

Hugh gave her a reassuring smile whilst resisting the urge to throw his cane at her for calling him a common detective. He would love to be a common detective, it would be a lot more bloody peaceful.

"You see, back when I was young. I, well—"

Fanny had stopped her pacing and moved up next to Lady Campbell, the young girl sensing scandal. If there was one thing Fanny loved more than scaring Hugh, it was gossip.

Hugh nodded encouragingly to Lady Campbell.

"My family owns a large amount of property in and around Edinburgh. Back in my younger days, one of our homes was known for the extravagant dinner parties my mother and father would host for the elite and wealthy of Edinburgh. My mother and father, god rest their souls, really knew how to host a grand dinner party. The parties were always very formal, civilised events where the most scandalous thing you would see was a man wearing the wrong shade of tartan."

She paused, swallowing, the sagging skin around her neck jiggling. "But you see, one year, back when I was eighteen, I hosted my first dinner party at the estate. Only I didn't have Mother and Father there to help as they were travelling abroad. Nor did I have hold of their contact list. So, my first dinner party turned into less of a formal dinner party and more of a, well, party."

To hear teenagers even took advantage of their parents being away to throw a party back in those days was surprising to Hugh. But teenagers would be teenagers he supposed, no matter the era. Even Hugh had tried to throw a party in his parents' house a couple of times when he was young—those had been some beatings from his father after both.

"But what has this got to do with Charlie boy here?" he asked, pointing towards the Charles shaped ball still lying in the fetal position under a pile of books. He should probably check if the fool was still alive.

"Oh, you see detective, this has everything to do with Charles. The party, how can I say this politely—"

"I prefer facts to polite Lady Campbell, and you don't strike me as the type who cares about being polite."

"Quite. Well, as I said, things got out of hand. There were types at the party who were not used to being invited up to the Campbell estate. The locals." She said this with a dismissive wave of her hand, as if she was trying to flick something disgusting over her fingers. "Including one young man named Graham Martin."

"Martin. Oh, I recognise that name!" exclaimed Fanny, who had somehow sneaked herself onto the table next to Lady Campbell.

"Well done, Detective Archibald," said Hugh sarcastically, "don't mind her Lady Campbell. Please carry on."

Lady Campbell eyed Fanny wearily. "Yes. Well. This Graham Martin was a local farmer. A strapping young man with vibrant red hair. Quite a charming young man, given his status. Ruggedly handsome, one might say. I remember he had rather large hands."

She gazed off into the distance as if the memory of the man was playing right before her dead eyes.

Hugh tried to blink away the image of Graham Martin's large hands working their way across Lady Campbell's body.

Fanny giggled. "Did you love him, Lady Campbell?"

Lady Campbell turned to Fanny, her mouth wide open, spiders fleeing towards her ears.

"I did not, you silly girl. I married the love of my life, Lord Campbell, shortly after I met Mr Martin—in fact, less than a month after the party."

"Oh, I do apologise," said Fanny, putting her hands to her chest, "it's just, the way you spoke of him so lovingly, I would imagine I would only speak about my husband in such terms."

"I think," said Hugh, interrupting, "Lady Campbell may have only loved this handsome farmer for one night and after a lot of gin."

"Ooooo," said Fanny.

Lady Campbell did not respond.

"And does that make the man underneath this pile of books you were trying to club him to death with a descendent of yours?"

Lady Campbell pointed a crooked finger at Hugh. "Not of me, but of that lying ratbag Graeme!"

Hugh smiled, the picture of what happened becoming clear in his mind. "But, there was a child?"

Lady Campbell lowered her hand and her gaze. "I married Lord Campbell after the party, and we had my William shortly after. There is no proof Lord Campbell wasn't the father."

"But there is speculation?"

"This bloody book," said Lady Campbell, the book she had been holding in her hand thudded to the floor.

With a groan and worrying pain in his hip, Hugh reached down and picked up the book. Its cover, frayed at the edges, had a thin layer of dust across its surface obscuring the title. He wiped the cover clean and lifted the book closer to his face so he could read the title.

George Martin, What Could Have Been.

"Ah. Mr Martin wrote a memoir."

"Four hundred pages of lies."

Hugh turned the book over, feeling the weight of it in his hands. Four hundred bloody pages, another author who couldn't be succinct.

"I presume he has mentioned his night with you in here?" he asked.

"In horrifying detail," replied Lady Campbell.

"Oh, can I have a read?" said Fanny, reaching for the book. Lady Campbell brought her cane down on the girl's hand, and Fanny let out a yelp.

"You certainly cannot. It is vulgar nonsense."

"I can see why Charles here would want a copy of this. It might entitle him to a part of your family's fortune if William's father was a Martin."

Lady Campbell glared at Hugh, who raised a coddling hand.

"I said *if*," Hugh said, trying to keep the woman from erupting.

Hugh then brought his hand to his moustache and scratched at the thick grey hair. "But I don't get it. Why hasn't someone come forward before this? George's parents or grandparents. Surely this book has been around for a long time?"

"It has been published for a long time, but that doesn't mean there are any copies. Whilst I was alive, I secured all the copies and had them burned. Or at least I thought I had." She wrinkled her nose at the book in disgust.

"So, you came back to have the evidence destroyed," said Hugh.

"I dislike your wording detective."

"Well, that is what it looks like to me."

"I came back so that filth would not sully my name."

"I have always found a hint of truth to filth."

Lady Campbell fell silent.

"Lady Campbell, I told you I would help you where I could. I know being across this side of the veil is causing you pain, and I don't want that. I also know you would want me to burn this book to get rid of any evidence of your wrongdoing. Correct?"

Lady Campbell nodded and licked her lips, the thin tangle of spider's legs appearing briefly.

"But you will also know I cannot do that. As much as I hate rancid old used books like this, I cannot burn evidence. Especially evidence that may help a man, no matter how much of a pain in the arse he is. I'm sorry, I have my integrity, Lady Campbell."

Hugh leaned back on the stack of books and crossed his arms, satisfied with his stance and, more importantly, his speech.

"Since when?" asked Fanny.

Hugh ground his teeth. "Don't you start."

"Well, you said it yourself. The man is horrible. Imagine if he got hold of Lady Campbell's fortune? Do you think that would make him a better human?"

Hugh narrowed his eyes, wondering again what use the dead girl was. She was right, Charles Martin was a knob, probably always had been a knob and always would be a knob—an even bigger one with a fortune. But Lady Campbell was no saint herself, and was he really the man to burn books?

"No, I am sorry. I cannot allow this. Lady Campbell, I apologise, but I cannot destroy this book. I will keep hold of it for Mr Martin until he wakes up. He bought and paid for the book and it is therefore his property."

"Actually—" croaked a timid voice from the floor, "he hadn't paid me for the book yet."

Hugh looked to the floor and the booksellers' wide-open eyes stared up at him from under a pile of dusty brown books.

***

Half an hour later Detective Hugh McRath stood outside the second-hand bookshop with a book in his hand too large to stuff in his top pocket and £4 less in his wallet.

Hugh had agreed to buy the book once the bookseller had told him Charles had yet to hand over his cash. It meant Hugh did not need to destroy evidence, and it meant Lady Campbell was happy to travel back across the veil with the help of Fanny.

"Just remember detective, I will hunt you down if I find you have wronged me. That book and its contents stay with you until the grave," Lady Campbell had said as she faded out of sight, her dead eyes on him.

If Hugh had a pound for every time a ghost told him they would hunt him down, he would be more than able to cover today's £4 loss.

As for Charles Martin, he was still out for the count, but thankfully had a pulse. Hugh had asked the bookseller to call an ambulance before he excused himself, not eager to answer any questioning that may follow. It would piss Charles off when he found out what Hugh had done, but then Hugh was even more use to the living than the dead being pissed at him.

Hugh looked to the sky. The sun was peeking out from behind the grey clouds which had covered Edinburgh when he left his flat this morning. He breathed in the fresh air, clearing his lungs of the stench of the bookstore, even the metallic taste in the back of his mouth had gone.

Maybe it was time to enjoy that long stroll he had intended to go on this morning before his watch rudely interrupted him.

He lowered his head from the warmth of the sun and his eyes fell on the row of pubs on the Grassmarket. Or maybe he would go for a walk tomorrow.

Revenge for the Past

The name on the gold plaque outside the house on Dublin Street in the heart of Edinburgh read: Dr Malcolm Cowie. A name Detective Hugh McRath had hoped he wouldn't see again unless etched on a tombstone whilst he stood over the grave taking a long and satisfying piss.

He looked down at his watch again to make sure it was pointing to the correct house and he hadn't just got the wrong door.

Please let me have the wrong door.

The gold watch had a large face and a peculiar number of hands. One of which was pointing straight at the door Hugh had been trying to avoid since his ex-wife had died. Another hand spun consistently telling Hugh there was a supernatural being on the other side.

"Bastard watch."

He swallowed, the familiar metallic tang of the presence of the dead caught at the back of his throat.

He had not come near this house since Sarah had passed away. She no longer lived here, so why would he? But now his watch had dragged him back down this hill on a winter's afternoon, his cane keeping him from slipping on the black ice as the cold burrowed deeper into his injured hip with each limping step. His frown had thickened as he followed the watch's instructions, hoping it would point to one of the other posh flats in this part of Edinburgh's New Town.

But no. The bloody thing had stopped him right outside the one door he had been avoiding since Sarah had passed across the veil.

There was a part of him hopeful that beyond the door stood Sarah and she had called him here, wanting to see him one last time.

He had thought about this a lot on the nights alone in his flat, where he had slept on his couch every night since she had left. He hoped he would apologise for the way he had treated her while she was alive—the focus on his job in the police, his drinking and the lack of attention ultimately led her into the arms of Malcolm. He hoped the words he found wouldn't taste as bitter as he still felt.

Another part of him would be resentful if Sarah had crossed the veil and chosen this home to visit first. This wasn't their home. This wasn't the home where they had raised their daughter Karen together. Why would she come here? It had been hard enough when she had left him when she was alive, but to choose his former friend Malcolm again, well, Hugh wasn't sure if he could take that.

Hugh also felt what he always felt when he was about to meet the dead—a touch of terror. It takes a lot for the dead to pass across the veil and mess around with the living. Usually they end up looking the worse for wear because of it, Hugh had seen some hideous sights in his time. He wasn't sure he was ready to see Sarah looking anything other than the perfect image he clung to in his mind.

Hope. Jealousy. Fear.

That was a lot of feelings for one Scotsman to feel on a Thursday afternoon. Normally Hugh only had room for one —anger.

A car horn beeped on the street behind him, waking him from his trance.

Hugh grumbled and stepped forward, wrapping his thick fist on the door.

There was a long pause and for a moment Hugh thought the house was empty and he could avoid the awkward encounter with the man he hated so much.

But then the slow shuffling of feet came from beyond the door. Someone was home.

Hugh cursed and chewed on the inside of his cheek, trying to prepare the surge of anger he could feel bubbling inside of him.

A lock clicked on the door before it was pulled open just enough for a thin slip of dim light to appear.

A head appeared in the gap. The enormous head of Dr Malcolm Cowie. Much to Hugh's delight, the man's face looked gaunt; his cheeks looked sucked in and he had sagging grey bags under his eyes. His wiry hair and eyebrows were also wild and unkempt. A film of sweat covered the surgeon's face. Was this the same man who used to wipe down seats in the pub before he sat in them?

Malcolm stared blankly at Hugh and asked, "What is it?" His tone impatient.

"Hello, Malcolm."

Malcolm frowned at Hugh, his giant, stupid forehead creasing. Hugh pushed down the urge to lamp in his head with his fist.

"Hugh. What are you doing here?"

Hugh was wondering the same thing.

"Can I come in?"

Malcolm blinked, then glanced over his shoulder.

"Now's not the right time."

Of course. The dead were inside. Maybe even Sarah. Malcolm would definitely not want Hugh to come in if Sarah was there. He would want to keep her to himself.

"I promise it won't take long," said Hugh, taking a step towards the door.

Malcolm's bony arm shot out from the door, blocking Hugh's path, a blue dressing gown sagging to his elbow.

"I'm sorry Hugh. I am just about to head out. Any other time. I would love to invite you in. I would," he looked almost sincere when he said this.

"Malky. You've still got your dressing gown on at 3pm on a Thursday."

Malcolm lowered his arm and pulled the dressing gown tighter around himself. He pushed the door closed until only his sweating, beaky nose was poking out through the gap.

"Yes, well, I was just about to get dressed—"

"Come on Malky," said Hugh, stepping towards the door.

"Stay back!"

Hugh froze. What was wrong with this fool? The man was always so assured of himself—a pompous twat. But he seemed scared here and Malcolm was never scared around Hugh, even when Hugh had him by the throat, back when they were having a "disagreement" over Malcolm's relationship with Sarah.

"Normally, I wouldn't piss on you if you were on fire, but I'm concerned Malky. Have you got company?"

"No. Absolutely not. No one is here. I'm all alone as always."

Malcolm's attitude tempted Hugh to turn and walk away, leaving Malcolm to deal with whatever was turning him into a shell of his old pompous self. But his watch had led him here, so there was something Hugh had to deal with on the other side of the door. He also knew Sarah wouldn't want him to leave Malcolm to suffer, no matter how tempting it was.

Sarah.

His stomach flipped again.

"I don't believe you Malky."

Malcolm's eyes bulged. "Stop calling me Malky. It's Malcolm. And why should I care whether or not you believe me?"

There was the old, pompous Malcolm.

"Also, it's none of your business anymore whether I am alone. You are no longer a police officer and Sarah isn't here, is she? Thanks to you."

Hugh almost crushed the handle of his cane.

"You little shit. How dare you speak to me like that?"

Malcolm's face collapsed. "I'm sorry. I apologise."

"Too fucking right you apologise."

Malcom looked into Hugh's eyes, his own now tear filled.

"I shouldn't have said that," his voice trembled as he spoke, "I am fine, Hugh. Please. Leave me alone."

Malcolm closed the door on Hugh's face. The scrapping of a lock clicking shut came from the other side.

"Twat." Hugh wasn't sure if that was aimed at himself or Malcolm. It felt appropriate either way.

He stood staring at the door, the blood pounding in his ears. Part of him wanted to put his fist through it, the other part wanted to turn and walk away. Malcolm was just a trigger for too many painful memories. Memories Hugh kept locked behind a door in his mind as much as possible.

Hugh didn't think he would ever be ready to face what was behind that door.

A face melted through the door. A face contorted in a hideous brown stained grin; blood dripped from a wound hacked out of its forehead.

"Jesus fucking Christ!" Hugh staggered back, barely stopping himself from falling to the pavement.

"Afternoon, detective. Did one know there is a ghost in the residence?" The voice of Fanny Archibald, a 15-year-old murdered in the mid-19th century with a butcher's knife to the skull, back to scare the shit out of Hugh for fun. Oh, and help the dead transfer back across the veil.

Hugh leaned on his cane, trying to gain his composure. "I gathered that. I just didn't realise it was your creepy arse."

Dressed head to toe in the black dress she was killed in, Fanny put a grizzled hand to her chest, "Oh, it's not just me, there is a lovely chap inside who is quite upset."

"By lovely chap, do you mean the twat in the dressing gown? Because I can assure you, he is not a lovely chap."

"Well, if you mean the man cowering in his living room, then yes. He seems quite upset with the presence in the house."

Hugh sighed and stepped to the door.

"No offence, but your lot tends to have that effect on people, Fanny. Who is in there with him?"

"I have not engaged with *my lot,* as you so eloquently put it. They have yet to reveal themselves."

"But there is definitely something in there with Malky?"

"Someone. We are not things."

"For fucksake. You know what I mean."

Hugh thumped on the door, his heart beating almost as loud as his fist against the wood. He realised he was excited, not about saving Malky but the thought of who the ghost might be.

"Malky, open up!"

"He won't open. He is quite upset. He seems to be muttering about being left alone. I can't think why, it is always nice to have company."

Hugh sighed and, not for the first time, wondered why he wasn't retired, lying on a beach letting the hot sun soak his white gut whilst he worked on drowning his liver in a steady stream of drink. But no, apparently, he was destined to deal with the dead and all the ugly past of Edinburgh, including his own.

Taking a step back from the door, he scanned the doorstep for likely hiding places for a spare key. Years in the police had taught him the public were pretty trusting and therefore stupid when it came to leaving access to their front door lying around. He hoped Malcolm was as stupid.

With a groan, he bent down and lifted the black rubber doormat sat in front of the door—no key. Straightening and ignoring the complaints of his back, he reached up and slid the handle of his cane across the top of the doorframe—still no key. Turning, he scanned the rest of the doorstep. Maybe Malcolm wasn't as stupid as he thought.

His gaze fell on a couple of withered plants in chipped pots on the steps leading back to the pavement. He smiled and lifted the first pot to find a silver key winking up at him. Lifting the key, he turned back to the door and placed it inside the lock.

"Breaking and entering now, are we?" said Fanny.

"Shut it you. I'm saving his life."

"What a hero."

The door lock clicked open and Hugh pushed the door in with a creak. Inside, the hall of the house was shrouded in darkness.

Hugh stepped inside, Fanny following closely behind—a loud scream greeting them as they entered the home of Dr Malcolm Cowie.

The step creaked under Hugh's foot as he moved towards the shrieking and moaning coming from behind the bathroom door at the top of the stairs in Malcolm's Dublin Street flat.

He held his watch up, the green glow from its face acting as a guide. At his age, having a tumble down the stairs had the potential to put him on his back for weeks. The light glimmered against pictures frames lining the wall of the spiral staircase—Hugh focused on the next step in front, worried he might glance over and see a picture of his ex-wife cuddled up to Malcolm. He might just throw himself down the stair if he saw that.

Hugh could feel the cool of Fanny's presence behind him as he worked his way one creaking step at a time towards the wall shaking cries. When he had first burst through the front door of the house, Hugh had thought the moaning had been

Malcolm, but they found the surgeon curled up on the coach in the living room, his hands covering his ears as he rocked back and forth.

The state of Malcolm and his home had shocked Hugh. Malcolm, the most fastidious man he had ever met, was sitting in nothing but a stained dressing gown and underwear, his pale sagging flesh on display as he struggled to control his breathing. The place stank of stale food and sweat, with the grand living room made to look like the inside of a full dishwasher that someone had forgotten to turn on.

But Hugh had no time or sympathy to do the dishes for that bastard Malcolm. He had a ghost to deal with. The moaning, which seemed to live in the bones of the house, had dragged Hugh to the stairs and towards the bathroom door he and Fanny were inching towards now.

The flush of a toilet came from behind the door.

"Do ghosts shit?" whispered Hugh.

"One does not like to discuss such vulgar topics, thank you very much." said Fanny.

Hugh rolled his eyes and kept moving up the stairs. He had seen some ugly things in his time between the decades in the police force and his time dealing with the dead, but he dreaded to think what mess a ghost could do with enough anger and a dirty toilet.

He really wasn't in the mood for shit covered walls.

"Is that Sarah?" said Fanny, jerking Hugh from thoughts of the stench awaiting him on the other side of the bathroom door.

He looked back at Fanny, who gazed at a framed picture on the wall at the top of the stairs through her dead eyes.

Hugh lifted his watch towards the picture, its green glow highlighting a pair of kind hazelnut eyes he saw most nights when he closed his own. The crow's feet around Sarah's eyes were deeper than when they had been husband and wife, but her smile seemed more joyful than any he could remember her flashing towards him.

The image was quite staged with Sarah sitting in a leather high-backed chair whilst Malcolm leaned stiffly against it. Despite the set-up, Sarah still managed to exude the type of relaxed, welcoming elegance which made her such a presence when she was alive. Malcolm, meanwhile, had all the relaxed charm of a ticket warden.

Hugh's chest ached as he looked at Sarah smiling towards the camera, out of the frame and into the depths of his grief. He leaned heavily on his cane and grunted back the pain.

Fanny took this as a response to her question. "Well, she was quite stunning, wasn't she."

"You sound surprised," said Hugh.

"Well, the two gentlemen in her life are hardly what you would call handsome."

"Cheers. Although, I won't be too offended since it's coming from the girl with half her skull split open."

Fanny turned her dead gaze to Hugh. "One should not assume any offence. I was just stating the facts."

Only a lady of the 19th century could call you an ugly bastard and then say it was your fault for taking offense, thought Hugh.

"Anyway," he said, "Sarah wasn't interested in looks. It was beneath her, all that. If you could make her laugh and listen to her, then that was what mattered to her more."

"I can see why she left you," said Fanny, her face breaking into a grin which Hugh could almost call cheeky if it wasn't so hideous.

"Now I am offended," said Hugh, grinning back.

"Revenge!" cried a guttural voice from behind Hugh, causing him to jump.

He turned back to face the bathroom door where the moan had come from.

Revenge. That couldn't be good. The voice had been male, though—nothing like Sarah. Unless she had undergone a sex change in her afterlife, in which case he would have to have a strong word with Malcolm.

"Our guest sounds upset," said Fanny.

"Don't they always," replied Hugh.

He stepped forward and pushed open the bathroom door with his cane.

Inside, the small bathroom was tiled from floor to ceiling in black and white square tiles, which were not smeared in shit—much to Hugh's relief. A toilet faced towards Hugh and to its right was a sink with a small cabinet above it.

There was a thin film of water on the floor, which Hugh's brogues splashed in as he stepped into the room. The metallic taste of the dead was almost overpowering. The hairs on the back of Hugh's neck stood up as he waited for the apparition to show itself. The freaky gits tended to jump out on you when you least expected it.

"Where is it?" he asked Fanny.

"Maybe, if you showed at least a touch of manners, then our friend would appear."

"Ok. Fine."

Hugh lifted his chin and opened his arms out as if addressing an audience.

"Please, can you come out? You disgusting arse barnacle," he called out, his voice echoing off the tiled walls.

"Delightful."

Hugh let out a laugh, but the room's lights quickly cut his laugh off as they flickered on and off. The brief glimpse of white light hurt Hugh's eyes, making him blink until only the green glow of his watch filled the room.

Then the gargling and rumbling of the walls began again. Only now, inside the room, it felt as if Edinburgh was suffering from an earthquake and the house was about to come tumbling down around them.

Hugh staggered forward, grasping at the sink to steady himself.

Then the toilet flushed. Only the water didn't disappear down into the pipes. It exploded out in a tidal wave of water.

"Fucking hell," Hugh cried, reeling back as the water shot past him towards the ceiling. He swung his cane back and smashed it into the cabinet on the wall, pulling the cabinet and its contents on top of him as he fell back.

He landed with a splash and a thud on the tiled floor, a shooting pain ran up his hip.

A groan escaped his lips. That was going to hurt in the morning.

"Revenge!" came another cry, filling the room.

Hugh lifted his head from the wet floor and looked towards the toilet.

A hand appeared over the rim of the toilet, its skin a sickly yellow. Another yellow hand appeared and slowly a man's head emerged from within the bowl. The skin on his face looked just as ill as his hands, the yellow even finding a way to cover his eyes. The man pulled himself up to reveal a bloated mass of a body. Hugh had seen similar dead bodies in his past, but usually it was those exposed to the sea for long periods, not toilet water.

The man wore some kind of hospital gown. Someone had cut the gown open at the waist to reveal the man's stomach, which had also been cut open to reveal his insides, a jumbled slimy mess of organs which were sitting on the toilet seat in front of him.

"My goodness, that is quite disgusting," said Fanny.

Hugh agreed as a wave of nausea threatened to overpower him.

"Revenge!" cried the ghost from his toothless mouth, his voice a gargling cry like he was swishing toilet water around his throat.

"Alright, for fucksake," said Hugh, "but did you have to cover me in toilet water."

A cackling laugh came from Fanny from the door behind Hugh. Clearly, she had enjoyed the whole show. This was going to be added to the never-ending list of fuck ups she liked to mock him about.

"And you stop laughing," he shouted towards her.

The girl stopped the cackling, but Hugh could still hear a muffled snigger from behind the girl's hands.

"Revenge. Revenge and penance!" cried the ghost.

Bloody ghosts. Always me, me, me with that lot.

"Shut and up. Try that first," said Hugh, rolling onto his side and feeling the toilet water seep through his shirt.

Hugh grabbed hold of the sink and pulled himself up. As he stood there was a rattling as several objects fell to the tilled floor.

He looked down to see the floor covered with white capped pill bottles.

Frowning, he bent down and picked up a bottle and studied the label.

"Revenge! There must be revenge!"

"How about a cup of tea first?" Hugh said, grinning at the ghost.

With a squelch underfoot and somewhere in his underwear, he turned away from the ghost and back towards the bathroom door, clutching the pill bottle in his hand.

He had some questions for the doctor of the house.

***

Hugh slurped his tea. He would have preferred something with a bit more bite, but he supposed this would do for now.

He sat in the living room in a leather chair opposite Malcolm, a towel under his backside to soak up some of the water weighing down his trousers. Still slumped on the couch, his chin almost touching his exposed chest, Malcolm hadn't looked at Hugh since he came back downstairs. Despite the chill in the room and his cold clammy clothes, the sight of Malcolm looking so downcast was enough to make Hugh feel all warm and cosy inside.

Whistling while he worked, Hugh had found a couple of reasonably clean cups and rustled up cups of tea for himself and his former friend. Fanny, meanwhile, had coaxed the ghost that had covered Hugh in toilet water downstairs with the promise of revenge. They both now stood like children in front in their headteachers' office waiting to be told off. Fanny, with blood pouring from the wound in her head and this new acquaintance with his guts swinging from his open stomach. The sight would normally make Hugh feel uncomfortable, but the thought of making Malcolm's night even more miserable made him smile and he turned to the wreck on the couch opposite him.

"So Malky," he said, shaking the pill bottle in his hand, "care to explain?"

The leather couch squeaked as Malcolm shifted and stared down at his untouched cup of tea.

Hugh persisted with glee, "Come on. Spit it out. Otherwise, he won't leave you alone?"

"Who won't?" said Malcolm, raising his red-rimmed eyes to Hugh.

"This guy here in the hospital gown with his guts hanging out," said Hugh, pointing to the ghost he knew Malcolm wouldn't be able to see.

"How rude. He can't help that," said Fanny.

"I don't know what you are talking about," said Malcolm.

Hugh sighed. "Don't tell me you haven't noticed. The rattling pipes, the moaning, the blockage in your bathroom. You've got a ghost and we are going to need an explanation, otherwise the ghost won't leave you alone and as much as I would like to leave you to slowly go off your head, Fanny here would resent me for it."

"Who is Fanny?"

"Detective Archibald," said Fanny, stepping towards Malcolm, her hand outstretched.

"Fanny put your hand down, he can't see you. You are a fucking ghost."

Fanny glared at Hugh.

"Hugh, have you gone quite mad? You are shouting to a room that is otherwise empty bar us," said Malcolm.

Hugh turned back to the doctor and shook the bottle of pills in his hand again.

"Don't change the subject, old boy. Me and Fanny here found you shaking like you've just come off a two-week bender and you've got a bathroom cupboard with more drugs in it than Scarface."

Malcolm turned his gaze back down to his cup of tea.

Hugh took a slurp of his own, the warm liquid doing nothing to clear the metallic taste of Fanny and her new friend. Not to worry, he would have a celebratory drink later.

"So," he said, "why would a dead man come back across the veil to make your life hell? I mean, personally, I could understand why I'd want to make your life hell. I've got a list as long my arm in fact, let me read it out—you're a pompous cunt, your eyebrows are too bushy, you are unnaturally skinny for someone your age, you dress like a smelly old professor, you—"

"Hugh, that is quite enough," said Fanny.

"Some of us don't work on our girth like you do," snapped Malcolm.

So, there was life in the old prick yet, thought Hugh.

Malcolm continued, "That doesn't mean there is someone from the dead out to get me. As a man of science, I find the notion frankly preposterous."

Hugh pointed his finger towards the ghost stood next to Fanny.

"What's your name?"

The ghost glared at Hugh with wide yellow eyes and bellowed, "Revenge!"

"Brilliant," said Hugh. Trust the ghost to suck the enjoyment out of his own moment of revenge.

He looked at Fanny. "Can you help?"

Fanny turned to the man, placing a hand on his shoulder. She stood on her tiptoes, the bottom of her dress coming off the floor to reveal her scabbed feet as she whispered in her fellow ghost's ear.

Hugh was always thrown off by how gentle the girl was with the other ghosts, no matter how violent or hideous they were around her. A 15-year-old with more patience than he ever had.

She turned her head to the side and the man bent down and whispered in her ear, his guts swinging from his stomach pressed against the side of Fanny's dress.

She nodded, then looked towards Hugh.

"His name is Billy Welsh," she said with a smile.

"Billy Welsh," repeated Hugh.

"Revenge," said Billy, nodding.

"You recognise that name?" asked Hugh to Malcolm.

Malcolm pulled his dressing gown around him and sat up straighter in his seat, as if finally remembering who he was.

"Yes. Although I do not see what he has to do with anything?"

"Who was he?" said Hugh.

"He was a patient. Liver transplant. Badly damaged because of cirrhosis after a lifetime of heavy drinking. I'm surprised you haven't needed one yourself."

Hugh ignored the dig and looked at Billy again. That would explain the yellow skin and the bloated body. The drink did that to you. The sight was almost enough to put him off pints of heavy. Almost.

"So, what happened?" he asked Malcolm.

"It is a very complicated operation. Especially for a liver so damaged as that one."

"So, he died on your table?"

Malcolm lifted his jaw. "All procedures have some degree of danger, and this is no exception. We cannot guarantee at the hospital everything will turn out ok. We are not miracle workers."

Hugh thought of his Sarah lying in the hospital, her eyes closed. A crisscross of wires and all the warmth sucked out of her as the doctor told him there was nothing they could do.

"Oh, I know that."

"That's not fair," said Malcolm, clearly understanding what Hugh was thinking.

He was right; it wasn't fair, but Hugh wasn't sure Malcolm deserved fair.

"So, Fanny, why is our boy so angry?" said Hugh, turning back to the ghosts.

The girl whispered into the ear of the bloated ghost again, who responded. The girls' eyes widened before she glared at Malcolm.

"Billy tells me our Dr Cowie performs his procedures whilst heavily medicated."

Hugh lifted the bottle of pills and gave it a shake.

"Was there an investigation into Billy's death?" he asked Malcolm.

"Of course. The medical board carried a full enquiry out. They dragged me in front of the board and questioned me."

Dragged. Hugh liked Malcolm's choice of word. The man never thought he was to blame for his wrongdoing.

"And the result?" asked Hugh.

"I was found to have done nothing wrong. The patient's death was just a terrible accident."

"Did they carry out a drug test as part of the investigation?"

Malcolm shifted in his seat.

"I am not sure what this has to do with you?"

He's deflecting, thought Hugh.

"I was called here by Billy Welsh. It's my job to help him across the veil, otherwise he will be stuck in this place forever and trust me you do not want that."

"Revenge!" cried Billy, beating his chest, and then pointing at Malcolm.

Hugh ignored the outburst.

"Now, to help a spirit, I need to understand why they are here. They are always here for a reason. Billy isn't just annoyed you were part of his death. He wants to make sure it doesn't happen to anyone else."

"Revenge!"

"It sounds more like he wants revenge, detective?" said Fanny.

Hugh glared at Fanny. "I am the detective in charge here Fanny, and I know what they need. Billy does not actually want revenge—"

"Revenge!" The pipes in the old house groaned with the ghosts' cry.

"I mean, he is literally saying it," said Fanny.

Whilst Hugh had been arguing with Fanny, he hadn't noticed Malcolm get up off the couch. When he turned back to face him, the man was lunging towards Hugh, his hands reaching for the pill bottle.

Hugh lifted his cane and rammed it into the surgeon's stomach, holding him back like a circus conductor controlling a lion with a chair.

Malcolm snarled and swung a hand towards the pills.

"Give me them. They are mine!"

Hugh closed his hand around the pill bottle and pulled it away from the wide-eyed doctor.

"Not until you explain Malcolm," said Hugh, through gritted teeth, "how long have you been on these?"

"It's not a problem!"

"Look at you," Hugh's voice softened, "what would Sarah think?"

Malcolm's body sagged over the end of Hugh's cane.

"Don't say that," he said, his voice now a whimper.

"I'm sorry, but as much as I like to see you in this much pain. I know *my* Sarah; she would not want to see you like this."

Malcolm shrank back to the couch.

"What is going on?" asked Hugh.

"I miss her, Hugh."

Hugh shifted in his seat. The wet cold of his clothes suddenly feeling a lot more uncomfortable.

"After she passed away," continued Malcolm, "I threw myself into my work. Taking on as much as I could. Anything to avoid coming back to this place. There is just too much of her here. Every time I set foot in the door, I expect to hear her voice call out asking how my day was or if I was ready for a G&T."

The woman did love a G&T, thought Hugh. He hadn't touched the stuff since she passed, the drink a direct link to too many memories he no longer wanted to taste.

The confession was pouring out of Malcolm now. "But the work eventually caught up and I started to self-medicate. Not much at first, I understood the medication of course. So, I took just enough to keep me focused. And it worked perfectly well to begin with. I could work longer hours than I ever had, and I could avoid this place. But then—then I needed a little touch more to keep me going."

Hugh knew where this was going. He had heard this so many times before and even though it was Malcolm, a weight pressed down on the back of Hugh's skull as he listened to the familiar tale.

"I thought I had control over it. I am a doctor, after all. I understand the advantages and risks of everything we prescribe."

"But you weren't prescribing the medication."

Malcolm nodded. "Quite. The thing with stimulants you see, is your body adapts. You need more than what you had before to have the same effect and I just kept taking more."

"And Billy Welsh?"

Malcolm rubbed his eyes. His palms came away to reveal tear-filled eyes.

"I had worked too many hours by the time the patient was lying on the table. Too many back-to-back shifts. Taken too many of those to keep me going,"—he said, eying the pills in Hugh's hand, his white tongue licking his top lip—"but there he was lying in front of me and, well, I couldn't say no, could I?"

"Why not?"

"Because it's my job Hugh. There are expectations of someone like me to perform. My patients and my staff would be—disappointed."

"So, you carried on?"

"I did," he said, raising his chin towards Hugh.

"And what went wrong?"

"You have to understand with liver disease as severe as this patient—"

"Billy," said Hugh, correcting the doctor.

Fanny nodded her approval.

Malcolm frowned and continued, "Liver disease as severe as his can lead to massive haemorrhaging when the damaged liver is removed. This is fine if you catch it quick enough and close the wound. But I—"

He paused, rubbing his hands through his hair, and staring blankly across the room.

Hugh let the silence sit in the room. Only he could hear the gargling breath of Billy.

Malcolm eventually continued, "The withdrawal from the drug I was taking had kicked in, and I didn't move quickly enough. Then I panicked and...well panic is the last thing you want in surgery. I am supposed to be the centre of the storm, no matter what is raging on around."

Malcolm shook his head, as if he was coming back from a trance. He turned to Hugh and met his gaze.

"There was an investigation. I was cleared you know, by a board—"

Hugh shook the bottle pills in his hand, silencing Malcolm. "Yes, but did the board of your buddies have all the evidence to hand?"

Malcolm didn't answer.

"Didn't think so. And that's the problem, you see. If the dead feel hard done by and are willing, they will come across the veil to get their revenge."

"Revenge!" cried Billy.

"Aye alright Billy, that's plenty from you."

"You really can see him?" asked Malcolm.

"Unfortunately."

"If you can see the dead, why don't you bring back Sarah?" said Malcolm, his voice quivering.

Hugh let out a sigh and looked towards Fanny.

"I wish I could. But you must understand that coming back across the veil is not natural. It is a painful experience for the spirits and every moment on this side of the veil can eat away at them."

Fanny chewed at her bottom lip and turned her gaze to the floor.

Hugh continued, "But some are willing to take the pain if it means resolving something even more painful from their life."

"So, Sarah, has nothing worth returning for?" said Malcolm.

"No, she has Karen. But Karen never caused her any pain."

"Only you did that," said Malcolm.

It was a cheap shot, but the cheap shots always have the sting of truth to them.

Hugh shrugged. "I also gave her the thing she loved the most—Karen. But if she was going to return, it would be to right some terrible wrong and Sarah was never one to look back with hatred."

"No, she wasn't," admitted Malcolm, "I miss that optimism."

"Yes, she was some woman, and that is how I want to remember her. If I saw her in this state, it would sully my memories of her," said Hugh, nodding at Billy.

"Now what?" asked Malcolm.

Hugh eyed the pill bottle in his hand.

"You know she wouldn't want me punished," said Malcolm.

Hugh glared at Malcolm. If he thought he could use Sarah as a bargaining tool, he was in for a rude awakening.

"But you do what you have to do, Hugh," said Malcolm, lowering his gaze.

"Revenge?" asked Billy, frowning, his gargling cry coming out as a question instead of a statement for a change.

"I'll speak to Karen," said Hugh, "she will know what to do next." Hugh's daughter had followed her father into the police force and was now a Detective Inspector. She would have neither the interest in this case or speaking to her drunk of a Dad. But Hugh could try, nonetheless.

"If you think that's best," said Malcolm.

"Revenge," said Billy with a toothless smile on his face.

***

"Morning!" shouted Fanny.

Hugh's hand jerked, the cup of tea spilling over the rim of the cup onto his hand.

"For fucksake!" he shouted and sucked the burning hot tea from his skin.

The elderly couple sat at the table next to Hugh in the coffee shop glared at Hugh.

He glared back.

"What are you doing in here? Oh Christ, there is not somebody in here dead, is there?"

They were sitting in a greasy spoon cafe just off the Royal Mile, close to Hugh's flat. The cafe served the best bacon rolls in the city and Hugh was sitting waiting on his order when Fanny appeared.

"Nobody is dead," Fanny eyed the two old women staring at Hugh, "soon maybe."

Hugh laughed. One of the old dears shook her head at him and they both turned back to their cups of tea.

"So, why are you here?" asked Hugh.

"One is here to see how you are doing after yesterday?"

"One is fine," replied Hugh. Which was a lie. He had spent most of last night drinking off the entire experience. The sight of Billy appearing out of the toilet. Having to face Malcolm again. Sarah smiling at him from the picture at the top of the stairs. All memories he wanted to wipe from his mind with the help of alcohol.

"Will your daughter be picking the surgeon up?"

"Is Billy back across the veil?" asked Hugh.

"He is. But that is not answering my question."

Hugh took a slurp of his tea, then placed the cup down on the table.

"Good interrogating, Detective."

Fanny smiled. "So?"

"I decided not to speak to Karen."

"I don't understand. Why not? I thought this was your chance?"

"Yeah, well, maybe I am getting soft in my old age."

"What? You?"

Hugh stared down at his tea. "I just didn't see the point. I'm not sure Sarah would have wanted me to anyway. And it's not like he took Sarah from me. I drove her away."

"Does this mean your relationship with the surgeon is rekindled?"

Hugh snorted. "Hardly. The man was pumping my wife for two years. All is not suddenly forgiven now she is dead."

"You have quite the way with words."

"Thank you, Fanny. I think that is the kindest thing you have said to me."

"One did not mean it as a compliment."

"I know."

"So, no one is any wiser about Malcolm's problems?"

"Nope."

"You know Billy will be angry if he finds out."

"*If* he finds out. I'm sure he will be blissfully happy once he passes across the veil. Like I told that prick Malcolm, the dead don't want to stay here, it's painful for them."

Fanny arched an eyebrow at Hugh, the wound on her head puckering open, spilling more blood down her cheek.

"You know I'm not going across the veil. I would miss you too much," she said.

"I know. A man can but try to find a little peace."

Barking at the Past

I pressed my wet nose against the pavement as soon as we stepped out the main door of our flat.

Sniff.

Delicious. Nothing like the smell of a dirty pavement.

I gave my soft and luxurious fur a shake. It was good to get outside and have a sniff, and to make sure none of the local bastard dogs had pissed on my territory. This part of Gorgie was my side of Gorgie and those fuckers need reminded.

But this was a little too late, and I had been comfortably lying tits up in front of the gas fire only moments ago.

The roads were empty, none of those rumbling box things on wheels in sight and my panting breath blew long puffs of white smoke into the night until they drifted up to the… ooooo twinkling lights in the sky! So shiny!

No, Charlie. Focus. Sniff your territory and mark it. Come on, you and your bladder have a job to do.

I give myself another shake, this time of night really was nippy on my nether regions. Frank must be off his head wanting to go out for a walk at this hour. But I won't complain, I've got lamp posts to piss on.

Speaking of which.

Sniff. Sniff.

Yes, my favourite post was nearby.

I pulled on my leash until it was taut, and my delicate paws scratched against the concrete.

I turned to Frank and gave him a savage stare with my bottomless brown eyes. You should have seen it. I can guarantee you'd be falling at my feet, begging for forgiveness.

But not Frank.

He didn't even look in my direction, scanning up and down the street with nervous twitches and glances. He hadn't even dressed himself properly for a night on the town, still wearing the comfy clothes I liked to lie on when he dared to leave me for the day. There was a bag in his hand, the type he usually carries when he was going to leave me for a long time.

Shit. Wait. I took a step towards him and let out a whine. He wouldn't leave me, would he? He wouldn't dare. Not after the last time, surely? He left me with the hideous woman he calls, "Mum". The one with hairs on her chin, who smelled too clean and thought she knew how to best look after me. She kept telling me to stay off the furniture. Well, I showed her, curling one out on her sheepskin rug then rolling in it. She had screamed down the phone to Frank about how she would never allow me back in her house and he could clean the shit off her rug.

My master peered down the dark street, his jaw set, bags under his eyes. He had been like this for days, no doubt caused by the despair at the thought of leaving me.

I sniffed the air and turned towards the lamppost again, staring at it longingly. Someone had definitely pissed on my territory. The musty smell in the air had nothing on my glorious scent.

Well, if I was going to be sent off again to live with that hag with the shit stained rug, then I would need to mark that post before I left. I wouldn't want the rest of the dogs around here thinking I had gone soft.

I let out a low whine. This usually works when I want Frank to listen to me or give me what I want. The combination of my incredible good looks and the cute whimper are hard to resist.

He reached down to scratch me under my chin, his hand shaking.

"You are such a handsome boy."

See, told you I was irresistible.

"But we need to go."

I licked his fingers; they tasted of salty sweat. *Delicious*!

He scratched me harder under my chin, just where I liked it. Staring down at me with red-rimmed eyes, he studied my short-wet nose, uniquely floppy ears, and my deep brown eyes (some would say they are protruding, but I know they are just jealous). Normally I would allow him to stare down at me adoringly, but tonight his bottom lip quivered as he took in every inch of my glorious pedigree. It was unnerving; I whined again and licked him under his chin, lapping up the salt from the rough surface of his unshaven skin.

"Come on, boy, we've got to go meet them, otherwise we'll be out on the street," he said, daring to draw his gaze from me. He frowned at the bag in his hand, then lifting his gaze to search the moonlit street opposite.

I swivelled my head to follow his gaze. Two eyes stared back at me from the darkness.

They were green, evil looking eyes and even through the gloom I could see they were watching me with disdain. They could only belong to one kind of animal—a cat. No other animal would look at you with such contempt.

Well, I would show the little shit.

I let out one of my fiercest barks. The monstrous cry echoed down the street.

The cat licked its paw.

So arrogant. Wait until I wrapped my jaws around its arse.

Frank froze, squeezing me tighter.

"Quiet Charlie," he said. I didn't like the way his voice shook. He must have spotted the cat as well.

Don't worry Frank, I will get the arrogant swine for the both of us.

I wriggled my chiselled stomach in his arms, twisting and turning, my breath panting into the night sky. He squeezed tighter.

"Hold still Charlie," he said, his voice rising.

But I had to catch the bloody cat for him. With an arch of my back, I pushed against his chest. His nails dug into my fur, but I broke free.

I landed with all the elegance of a packet of sausages being thrown in a frying pan. Thankfully, the rippling muscle in my sides cushioned my fall when I hit the pavement, the leash around my neck clattering against the concrete.

Rolling to my four paws, I turned towards the alleyway, searching the dark for the eyes of my arch nemesis. The glass orbs which had stared mockingly from the dark were gone. The coward must have run away to some dark hole.

I growled. A deep, impressive growl.

The smarmy git couldn't have made it far.

I shot towards the opening.

"No!" cried my master, his footsteps clattering on the road behind me.

Good. He would get to watch me chase down and capture the foul beast who mocked us.

But as I stepped towards the dark street, two giant bright lights appeared, temporarily blinding me.

I skittered to a halt and tried to blink away the white light behind my eyelids.

The rev of an engine filled the street.

I froze, my legs felt stuck in place.

Frank came up from behind and scooped me up into his arms.

At least that metal contraption would see the both of us. Although I am an impressive beast, some might call me short legged. All lies, of course, but the driver wouldn't have been able to see me in the street. I would be fine in my Frank's arms now though.

Surely.

Tyres screeched against the cobblestones. Beyond the white light, I could see a silhouette in the driver's seat.

I barked, trying to slow their approach. Didn't they see us standing in the middle of the road?

My master squeezed me tight, bracing us for the impact. I turned my head, burying my face into his chest, the familiar smell of his sweat filling my nose. I should have appreciated this smell more.

A screaming crunch filled my ears, and the world spun around me. The lights taking turns with the dark night sky to fly past my vision.

I was lying on something cold and hard. My fur soaking wet.

When did I end up on the ground?

Had it been raining?

My ears rang. I blinked my eyes open and the black sole of my master shoe appeared before my nose, light streaming across my vision.

Why was he lying down?

There was a slow rattling of a machine ticking over. A door creaked open. The clip of heels against cobblestones. Someone had come to save us.

I let out a whine of appreciation.

The ringing in my ears calmed down, and I could hear the sharp gasps of Frank's breathing. I tried to turn my head towards him, but for some reason I couldn't move my neck.

Strange, I had such a flexible neck normally.

The footsteps of our saviour came to a halt, their shadow blocking the light.

I breathed in the acrid smell of alcohol.

"Ssstupid prick," said the voice of a woman, her words coming slurred and messy, "think I'm shtupid don't you. Thought you could leave. Well now, look at you and your stupid fucking dog."

"I wasn't—" responded my master. His voice sounded like he was gargling water whilst he spoke.

I let out a whine. I wanted to crawl up onto his chest and give him a lick under his chin, but I couldn't get any part of my body to move.

My eyes slowly closed. I had let Frank down; I was too tired to save him here.

The golden brown contained within the glass Detective Hugh McRath held to his eye washed out the green of the fruit machine's lights as they flashed on and then off. On and then off.

On and then off.

He removed the glass from his eye and waited for the room to come back into focus. It was a long wait.

How much had he had to drink? Two pints of heavy in the first pub…three in the second…in the next, he started having whisky chasers. That was one, two, six…fuck it, a lot.

He must have had a lot if he ended up in here. The *Ghoul and Ghost,* his local boozer and only a couple of doors down from his flat in the Old Town of Edinburgh. Even being Hugh's local and given his passion for getting pissed, it was always a low point if he ended the night in here. There was too much danger of him bumping into the dead in this place —the pub seemed to be a revolving door across to the veil— the land of dead. Hugh had met more ghosts in this pub than anywhere else in Edinburgh and today he was fucking sick of ghosts.

A thick layer of dust clung to every surface, although he could see where his stuttering footsteps had staggered to the bar on the floor. Images of flashing ghosts covered the fruit machine, their mouths wide open in never-ending screams whilst they held wads of cash in their hands. The flashing colours made Hugh's right eye ache.

Fucking ghosts.

He lifted the glass to his lips, hitting the rim against his chin on its journey up. The whisky tasted like fire, leather and had all the subtlety of a smack to the chops. Hugh licked the drops he had dribbled into his moustache, the liquor burning his tongue but still not getting rid of the metallic taste in his mouth. Fucking ghosts. They even tasted horrid.

All day their presence had lodged at the back of his throat like a bad penny. He knew all the heavy and whisky in the world wouldn't get rid of the taste of them, yet he was twelve drinks in (no wait, fourteen?) and needed one more.

Hugh swivelled in his seat, his large gut pressing against the bar. The usual beauty of Sheila was missing from behind the bar tonight. The woman had all the personality and gentleness of a bulldog who had been kicked in the testicles. Sheila was more likely to tell you to fuck off than serve you. But at least she had personality. This barmaid standing in for her tonight, well, did not.

She stood staring off into the distance, mouth sagging open, jowls almost touching her tits. Hugh thought she may have been pretty in her youth (he doubted anyone would say that about him) but years of either fags, booze or life had slowly sucked the looks out of her. Her skin was grey and insipid, she had heavily painted eyes, but no amount of blue emulsion could cover up those bags. Bizarrely, she wore a low cut, sparkling purple dress as if she was just on her way to have a wild Christmas night out, not to stand and serve an empty pub with a face like a skelpt arse.

"Exshcuse me," said Hugh, slurring his words. The barmaid didn't even flinch and just stared into the distance.

"Er, said excuse me," he said, raising his voice, but the woman didn't move, her gaze unblinking at whatever was fascinating her over his shoulder.

He turned to look. On the wall was a mirror covered with stains, making it virtually impossible to see his reflection. He was grateful for that, knowing he probably looked like a steaming pile of shite. The stained reflection helped to blot away some of the barmaid's sagging skin. She almost looked —good. Christ, how much had he actually had to drink?

He turned back to the barmaid and waved his hand in front of her face.

"Anybody home?"

"She probably thinks you have had enough," whispered a voice in Hugh's ear.

He flinched and had to grab hold of the bar to stop himself from toppling over onto his back.

"For fucksake," said Hugh, his heart pounding in his chest.

"Sorry, did I scare you?"

He looked right, his vision blurred, but he could still make out the faded image of a young girl sat next to him. She had a grotesque smile plastered on her face, revealing a stained set of teeth. Dressed in a long black dress covering her from chin to toe. Hugh often wished her dress extended to cover her face as well, blocking out the disgusting gaping wound in her forehead. A butcher's knife had left the wound when someone slammed it into her skull in 1865. Who the murderer was, Hugh didn't know—Fanny Archibald wouldn't tell him. Apparently, it was rude to discuss a ghost's death. Well, that was a lie. All he ever did was listen to ghosts bleat on about their deaths.

"What do you want?" he grunted.

"Just here to keep you company."

"I don't want company. I've had enough of your kind of company for a day."

Fanny clucked her tongue. She didn't like him using the phrase, "your kind" to describe ghosts. But Hugh didn't care that she didn't like the term.

"Here, barmaid, another whisky now," Hugh said, turning away from Fanny.

The barmaid didn't move, she just kept staring at her reflection with the vacant look in her eye.

Hugh shifted in his seat and tried to get a better look at her through his blurred vision. Where was Sheila? Had she served him when he came in? He swallowed down the metallic taste in his mouth; the unease growing inside of him.

"I told you, the barkeep has decided you have had one too many drinks, detective. The lady is quite right as well. You stink."

Hugh looked around the bar. The place was dead. A little too dead for his liking.

"Where is Sheila?" He barked, "She'll get me a drink."

A snuffling whine came from Hugh's feet. He looked down.

Sat at his feet was a dog, the most hideous dog Hugh had ever seen. It stared up at Hugh through one protruding eye, the other flopping out of its eye socket and dangling around his chin. Clumps of fur were missing from the dog's back, revealing raw flesh, which seemed to squirm as if worms were crawling under the surface. Its jaw jutted out at an awkward angle and was clearly affecting the dog's ability to control its saliva as there was a bubbling puddle of drool at the dog's feet.

Hugh jumped up from his seat, sending the barstool clattering to the floor.

"Fucking! Creepy! Fuck—what the fuck is that?!"

"Ah, one has made a new friend today."

Fanny leaned down and scratched the hideous dog behind the ear. The dog whimpered through its deformed jaw in appreciation.

"His name is Charlie."

"He's dead."

"How rude of you to say."

"What does he want?" asked Hugh, eyeing the dog suspiciously. In Hugh's vast experience, the dead always wanted something—the selfish bastards.

"Well, I do not know, do I? Maybe he is just lonely and needs company."

Fanny ran her fingernails down Charlie's back, scratching at the angry looking exposed flesh.

The pints of heavy and whisky chasers in Hugh's stomach did a backflip.

"Well, I said I didn't need company so he can piss off," said Hugh, waving a dismissive hand at the dog.

"You know that is not how this works. There is a reason Charlie has decided to join us."

Hugh reached down and picked the bar stool backup and dumped himself on the creaking seat. He needed a drink even more now.

"Whisky," he said, slamming his hand on the bar. The barmaid didn't even blink.

"What is wrong with this woman? You're supposed to serve me drink, it's your fucking job."

"And your job is to help the dead," said Fanny.

"Well, maybe I don't want to anymore. Maybe I just want to be left alone. I didn't ask for any of this shit. The constant appearance of you lot with your never-ending demands. I've lost everything because of you—"

"Boohoo," interrupted Fanny, "do you think any of us want to be dead? Or to have our problems solved by someone like *you*?"

Hugh leaned in closer to Fanny.

"Well, you know where you can go don't you?" he said, through gritted teeth.

Fanny turned her gaze away. "You know one does not want to go across the veil."

"Well, *one* does not want to deal with your shit anymore."

A low growl came from below the bar.

Hugh looked down to see Charlie, his leg cocked, and firing a stream of piss across Hugh's brogues.

"You dirty bastard," said Hugh, kicking a leg out at the dog. Instead of the satisfying crunch of bone, his foot slipped straight through the dog's body. His toe connected with the hardwood of the bar sending a shooting pain up his leg alongside the familiar shiver caused by touching a ghost.

Fanny had her hands to her mouth and was giggling.

"Shut up you," said Hugh, holding his leg and wriggling his throbbing toes in his brogues.

Charlie hobbled over to Fanny and lifted his front two paws up to the girl's legs. She bent down and picked the dog up into her lap.

The dog sat panting, its eyeball hanging from its socket jiggling with every breath.

"There you are, you little shit," called a rattling voice from behind the bar.

Hugh turned towards the sound.

The barmaid was smiling now, with all two front teeth on display. A black beetle crawled out of her mouth and disappeared into her hair.

Hugh's breath caught in his throat. Of course. No wonder he wasn't getting another whisky—the barmaid was dead.

Charlie growled at the woman and barked.

"I do not think he wants to say hello," said Fanny, wrapping her arms around her new friend.

"You mind your business, you little bitch."

Hugh looked up at the woman, her face twisted in a vicious sneer. Her skin barely clung to her skull, her hair looked full of clumps of mud or flesh. How had he not spotted she was dead before now?

But it wasn't just the dead woman's features that were sobering, it was her demeanour.

She wasn't just dead.

She was dead and pissed off. Hugh always found that a particularly disturbing combination.

A wave of nausea swam across him. He was ready for his day to be over now, ready to pass out on his couch and await the hangover.

But no. The dead had found him again and wanted to play.

"Did you hear that detective? The way this woman spoke to me?" said Fanny.

"Careful," said Hugh. The girl tended to run off at the mouth around other ghosts and left Hugh to deal with the consequences. He was in no fit state to deal with consequences.

"Well," continued Fanny, undeterred, "I believe a woman should know her manners, and you appear to have forgotten yours."

"Who the fuck are you?" spat the dead barmaid.

Fanny drew herself up on the barstool, "I am Fanny Arch
—"

The barmaid interrupted her with a rasping cackle.

"Fanny! Your name is Fanny?! What kind of name is
that?"

Fanny pursed her lips and scratched at the wound on her
head. "A perfectly reasonable name, thank you very much."

The barmaid sneered. "No, a perfectly reasonable name is
Jackie," she said, stabbing a finger at her chest which jiggled
disturbingly, "where I come from a Fanny is well a *fanny*."
The finger she pointed to her chest turned down and pointed
to whatever was hiding under the bottom half of her
sparkling purple dress.

Hugh tried his best to push away thoughts of fanny from
beyond the grave.

"How crude! Where I come from, a woman must
remember her manners or at least learn to adjust them."

Jackie stepped forward, her eyes narrowing.

"And are you going to adjust them for me—*Fanny*?"

"Stay back," said Fanny, raising a hand, "or I will require
my gentleman friend to get involved and apprehend you."

"Leave me out of this," said Hugh and he leaned over the
bar and grabbed a bottle of whisky, screwed its top off and
took a long swig. It was not like Sheila was around to stop
him and he needed all the help he could get with these two.

The whisky burned at Hugh's throat, and the room swam
at the edges of his vision.

"That waster is too busy trying to join us than protect
you," said Jackie.

Harsh, but fair, thought Hugh.

"You really are a vile woman," said Fanny. "What are you doing here anyway? Take yourself away back across the veil at once."

"I'll go if he goes," said Jackie.

"Hey, I'm not dead yet lady," said Hugh, taking another draw from the bottle of whisky. Although he was trying his best tonight.

"Not you. Him," she said, pointing at the dog.

The dog growled in response; drool dripped from his chin onto the edge of the bar before hanging from the wood like a long swinging rope. Hugh swallowed down his disgust but tasted nothing but the familiar metallic tang of the dead.

"Charlie? You cannot take him. He wants nothing to do with you, thank you very much," said Fanny, pulling the dog tighter to her chest.

She turned to Hugh. "Detective, tell the woman."

Hugh wanted nothing to do with this argument, but he knew he couldn't just walk away. That was not how the dead worked.

With a sigh, he asked, "Why do you want the dog?"

"I don't want the bloody dog," said Jackie, her voice sharp, "but he came over here looking for his owner and somehow I've ended up with him."

"You knew his owner?" asked Fanny.

"Oh, I knew him alright," Jackie spat and reached into the bosom of her dress and pulled out a packet of *Embassy* fags. Hugh hadn't seen a packet of them in years. She slipped one into her cracked lips and lit up.

Hugh sighed inside. Why had he asked? He should have known where this was going. The dead and their fucking love lives, he was sick of it. Well, he wasn't asking what happened; he wasn't interested.

"What happened?" asked Fanny.

Hugh gave his nosy partner a look of disgust.

"Me and this mutt's owner had a thing back in the day," Jackie said, blowing a stream of smoke towards the ceiling of the pub.

"A thing? What do you mean by a thing?"

"Is this one for real?" asked Jackie, looking in Hugh's direction.

Hugh shrugged.

"We were shagging. You know, his cock was going in my fanny."

Fanny pulled her face away in horror, which, given how horrific her face looked, was quite a sight. Hugh enjoyed the look nonetheless; it was nice to have someone else wind the girl up.

"Yes. That's what you did back in the 80s, you frigid cow. Judging by what you've got on, you were from a more uptight time."

"I was born in 1850, a time when a gentleman was taught to respect a lady."

"Sounds fucking boring."

Jackie took another long draw on her fag before pointing at Fanny and the one-eyed companion in her lap who was panting, his loose eyeball bouncing up and down.

"But there is something to be said for the respect thing. Christ knows, I've known a lot of disrespectful men in my time. I thought this little shit's owner was different. Frank was his name."

She chewed at her nail as if the name was painful to speak before continuing, "I thought Frank was different. But no, he was just like the rest of them. Wanting to run away as soon as he got what he wanted from me. And normally I would let them leave as I knew they were after nothing but my body."

Hugh scrunched his nose up as he looked at the sagging grey flesh being held in place by a sparkling dress. Hard to believe anyone would be after Jackie for her body now.

"Well, that time it was different. I was too upset not to let the disrespect pass," Jackie said.

"What did you do?" asked Fanny.

"I taught him a lesson. He couldn't just run away and leave me. Not like that. Slinking off in the dark of the night with his dog under his arm."

"So, you..."

"Killed them both. The dog and this Frank," interrupted Hugh.

The barmaid nodded and took another puff on her cigarette.

"I hit them with my car when they were trying to run away."

"You monster!" cried Fanny.

After all the dead Fanny had helped him send across the veil, Hugh thought she would realise how hideous the living were. But no, she still held onto the notion that people rarely did horrible things to each other. It was almost sweet. Tragic, but sweet.

"Oh, don't give me that. I was heartbroken. I was drunk," said Jackie.

She stared at the glowing light of the end of her fag like she wanted to swallow it whole.

"It was a mistake," she said, her voice barely audible over Charlie's panting.

"But poor Charlie," said Fanny, scratching the dog behind his ear. Charlie leaned back and licked the girl under the chin, his tongue slipping out from the side of his deformed jaw.

"Look, you've got to understand," said Jackie, her voice missing some of its sharp edge, "I had never felt like that before. I thought—"

A bell clinked behind Hugh, cutting off Jackie. Hugh frowned and turned towards the sound just as the door to the pub slammed shut behind a tall man dressed in a tracksuit caked in blood and mud. He had covered his tracksuit with an overcoat more suited to a nice three-piece suit like the one Hugh had on. In his hand, he carried a brown leather holdall. He was what Hugh would think women class as tall, dark, and handsome, if it wasn't for the fact blood was pouring out of his mouth and judging by the colour of his skin, he was quite clearly dead.

The infamous Frank, no doubt. But Hugh had been expecting him to make an appearance. What made Hugh frown was the sound of the bell. A bell on the front door was a bit welcoming for the *Ghoul and Ghost*. Hugh didn't think the usual barmaid Sheila would like the constant ringing in her pub. Unless she was using the bell to tell customers to fuck off before they even set foot through her door.

"You thought what?" asked the tall, dark, handsome, and very, very dead Frank.

"Frank—," said Jackie.

Charlie barked and Hugh turned to see him throw himself off Fanny, landing face first on the wooden floor of the pub.

His loose eyeball rolled across the floor until the cord attaching it to his eye socket pulled tight, preventing the eyeball from disappearing across the pub. Dragging himself to his feet, the dog skittered across the floor towards Frank.

Frank dropped the holdall, sank to his knees, and picked up the dog.

"Hello boy," he said, grinning, blood pouring out of his mouth. Charlie gave the man an affectionate lick on his blood-stained chin.

"What are you doing here?" asked Jackie.

"I think I'm here to see you," said Frank, turning his loving gaze to the woman on the other side of the bar.

"Me? What are you wanting? An apology? Well, you've come to the wrong bar."

"No. I've come to the right bar. Just like I did back in 1983. Remember?"

Jackie averted her eyes and took another draw of her fag.

"You spilt a drink down my denim shirt. Accidentally on purpose."

Jackie blew out the smoke, a smirk playing at the edge of her lips.

"I was going to kick off about the shirt being ruined," said Frank, "then I turned round, and it was you. Those eyes. That smile. That body."

Hugh poured himself another whisky. It was time to drink until the images of the dead and their love lives were drowning.

"I told my mate Harry that night I met the woman of my dreams and I would marry her one day."

"Oh, how romantic," said Fanny, her voice floating across the bar.

Was it? Hugh thought it sounded like the unrealistic expectations of a horny young fool.

"Except it was a load of shit, wasn't it?" said Jackie, throwing her fag to the floor and stomping on it, "you lied to Harry and to me. You tried to leave."

"I wasn't leaving. I was meeting someone else," said Frank, stepping towards the bar, Charlie curled up in his arms being carried like a prince.

"Oh, of course you were. Who was she?" said Jackie, glaring at Frank with her dead eyes.

"No, it wasn't like that. It wasn't a woman. It was—" Frank hesitated; his gaze no longer able to meet anyone's in the bar.

"It was who?" spat Jackie.

"Someone I was meeting to help with money."

"Money? What are you talking about?"

Frank sighed and lowered his head, blood dripped from his mouth. Charlie lapped at the steady stream, whining with appreciation.

Hugh gulped down some more whisky.

"I was making money on the side of my job at the bank," mumbled Frank.

"Doing what?"

"Drugs."

Fanny gasped. She was enjoying this, thought Hugh. The drama's the dead put on were part of the reason she hadn't moved across the veil yet. The girl enjoyed the entertainment far too much.

"Drugs?! You? Don't give me that, you were as strait-laced as they come."

Frank looked up at the woman, his eyes tear filled. "I didn't mean to. It was the spending. It was too much, and I didn't want you to think I had gone cheap—"

"Don't blame me."

"I'm not. I was…stupid."

"I don't understand. How did you even?"

"It was Harry. He got me connected with someone. I was just picking bags up for him and dropping them off at different locations," said Frank, and he nodded at the holdall on the floor, "nothing too serious, but I just couldn't tell you."

"So, all those times you said you were taking Charlie out a walk, I thought you were meeting some other woman. But you were just out doing that."

Hugh let out a snort. "Your dugs name was Charlie, and you were selling Charlie—"

"Quiet detective," scowled Fanny, "they are trying to sort out their relationship issues."

But the whisky had taken over Hugh's mind now and he roared with laughter at his joke.

"You are not funny," said Fanny, "we are supposed to be helping them."

"Christ, we need *Jerry Springer* for these two."

Fanny frowned, the wound on her forehead did the same. "Who is this Jerry Springer? Is he a priest or a counsellor of some kind? How can we get in contact with this man?"

Hugh groaned and tipped the bottle of whisky to his mouth again.

"So, you need to know I never would have hurt you Jackie," said Frank. Hugh turned to find the dead man closer to the bar now, both him and the dog giving Jackie a pleading look. Well, Frank was, the dog was staring at the floor with the swinging eye whilst the other protruding eye, still in its socket, stared at either Jackie or the ceiling.

Hugh's vision was no better than the dogs thanks to the drink, and he rested his chin on his hands trying to get the three ghosts in front of him to stop swimming.

"But I hurt you. I killed you both," said Jackie, her voice barely a whisper.

"It's ok. It was just a misunderstanding."

Hugh had seen some misunderstandings in his time, but running over your cheating lover (who wasn't actually cheating on you) and their dug was something else.

Frank didn't seem to care. "I should have been truthful with you, then we wouldn't be in this mess."

Jackie raised her head to Frank. Her eyes were full of hope, but Hugh could still see the trace of fear, like the hope was a metal trap with sharp teeth she was gently lowering her hand into. Hugh recognised the feeling well from his own disastrous love life. The trap had bitten down on him.

"But now what?" asked Jackie.

"You go with him," said Fanny, "you can be together across the veil."

Frank nodded. "Come with me. Come with Charlie. He brought us back together for a reason. Or do you need me to throw a drink over you this time?"

Jackie smiled, revealing the two hideous teeth left in her mouth. She took a tentative step forward before stepping through the bar and into Frank's arms.

They kissed, the long passionate kiss of two lovers reunited.

Charlie whimpered and then barked, clearly upset at the lack of attention.

Fanny let out a satisfied sigh next to Hugh.

Hugh threw back another nip of whisky.

The couple separated and turned to face their audience, both grinning ear to ear. Jackie's lips and chin were smeared with blood, giving her the look of a deranged clown.

Hugh slammed the bottle of whisky down, its contents gone.

"Sho wait a minute. He lied to you and shold drugsss on the side," said Hugh, with a slur, "she then ran you and your fucking dog overs because she…is a jealous fucking psssycho. Yet you want to spend the rest of eternity together across the veil with this one-eyed monster dog?"

"Isn't it marvellous!" said Fanny.

"Fucking ghosts," groaned Hugh, tipping forward, his head slamming onto the bar.

"Well, do you want another drink or no?"

Hugh mumbled and lifted his head. A blurred face swam in and out of his vision until slowly the image cleared to reveal the hard look of a familiar unwelcoming woman's face—Sheila. The *Ghost and Ghoul's* resident miserable barmaid.

Hugh swallowed, the taste of heavy and whisky coating his mouth. The room around him hummed with the din of contented drinkers.

He blinked, trying to gather his thoughts. How long had he been sitting here? Where was Fanny? What about Frank and Jackie? And that demon dog who pissed on his shoes?

The realisation hit him like a punch to the gut. The ghosts must have pulled him under when he sat down in this place. He had been too drunk to notice.

"Well?" grunted Sheila.

"Whisky," he said.

Fucking ghosts.

A Reflection of the Past

Detective Hugh McRath stood at the top of the plush staircase, his daughter by his side, her arms folded across her chest.

"Well, go on then," she said.

Hugh drummed his fingers across the brim of the black bowler hat he held to his ample stomach and eyed the staircase.

Despite the hour, he could see the thick carpet his brogues sunk into extend down into a room lit by an aggressive, bright light.

Lord knows, as a supernatural detective, he had descended into darker, creepier rooms in his time. The room below looked positively bright and airy compared to some tombs he had wandered through in the past.

But the supernatural knew their history, and there was plenty of that in this building.

Originally built as a hospital in the mid-19th century to help house and educate some of the poor children of Edinburgh, in the end, the building became known for taking in and educating the deaf.

With its multiple towers and never-ending sea of windows, the building looked more like a palace than a school. Even Queen Victoria eyed the building up for a swap deal with her own residence in Edinburgh back when she opened the hospital in 1850. It was one of Hugh's favourite buildings in the city.

But something this beautiful, this close to the city centre of Edinburgh, was always going to get snapped up by developers. Formally a place which housed the poor and uneducated, it had been turned into a building with an expansive foyer covered in thick luxurious carpets, club rooms where the chapel used to be and a concierge who gave you disapproving looks if you didn't own one of the overpriced apartments inside.

Oh, how the rich forget the past.

But the dead don't.

The peculiar watch on Hugh's wrist started getting excited as soon as he limped, with the help of his cane, into the grounds of the apartments. The middle of the three hands spinning, indicating supernatural beings were present. The long hand turned from noon and pointed him in the direction of the top of the stairs and by the side of his estranged daughter. Thankfully, the smallest hand on the watch had kept its mouth shut so far.

The metallic taste in his mouth and familiar tingle in his spine also gave Hugh the tell-tale signs when he found his daughter Karen (or DI Dunn as she liked to be called, especially by him) the supernatural were probably lurking at the bottom of the stairs.

But none of this was a concern. This was Hugh's job, after all. Investigate Edinburgh's never-ending pile of creepy shit and make it slightly less creepy.

No, the bigger concern about limping down those stairs was whether Karen would push him from behind once he was a few steps down.

Hugh pursed his lips, feeling the bristles of his thick moustache tickle his top lip. He glanced at Karen, the blue light of the panda car outside flashing through a window highlighting her stern face. The look in her eye just now told him the thought of dumping her dad headfirst down the stairs had crossed her mind.

Karen had tied her dark brown hair up, revealing the sharp, elf-like features of her mother. But she had Hugh's eyes, the blue diamond's only highlighting further how dark the bags under her eyes had become. Given she was a Detective Inspector and the mother of a two-year-old the bags weren't surprising. They only highlighted to Hugh how grown up his little girl was.

"You look well," said Hugh, lying.

"You look like you've put on more weight."

"Ouch. Got me there. I still love my healthy Scottish diet," said Hugh, slapping his gut under the three-piece suit desperately trying to hold the jingling mass in place.

"And the drink judging by your breath."

Double ouch.

That was uncalled for. Yes, Hugh had a few whiskies when she had called him. But what had she been expecting at 8pm?

Hugh pushed down the anger he felt bubbling under his skin at the jibe. That was no way to speak to your father, even one as useless as him.

Instead, Hugh tried changing the subject. "How's Eve?"

Karen's face softened briefly at the mention of her daughter, but she quickly recovered, her jaw clenching and her gaze turning hard.

"None of your business."

"That's not fair Karen, she is my grand—"

"No, she's not. A granddaughter is someone you visit. Someone who recognises your face and runs up and gives you a cuddle as they are excited to see you. You are a stranger to Eve."

Triple ouch.

"Karen—"

"It's DI Dunn. Now, I have asked you here to help with this investigation," she said, her voice turning formal and business-like, "we are looking for your *expertise* to help us. Can you take a look?"

Hugh looked towards the staircase and then back to Karen.

"I will take a look but only because my daughter is asking."

Karen rolled her eyes.

"But I have one thing to ask," said Hugh.

Karen raised an eyebrow, suggesting he may continue very, very carefully.

"If I do step down there, how do I know you won't kick your old dad in the arse and send him tumbling down the steps?"

The edge of Karen's mouth twitched like she almost wanted to laugh.

Laughter had always been the one thing he could count on as a parent when Karen was younger. She had the same sense of humour as her dad and the two of them used to giggle at each other's jokes. Much to Karen's mother's annoyance—she wasn't much of a fart joke fan.

Hugh pushed further, "Because if I break my neck it would be awfy difficult for me to keep up my exercise and healthy eating and drinking regime."

The brief peak of a smile melted. Her mouth a thin line again. He had pushed it too far and mentioned the D word. Karen didn't find Hugh's drinking habits amusing or his jokes about them. Who could blame her? Christ knows his love of drink had caused her enough trouble over her life.

"Dad, I've not got time for this."

Dad. Well, it was a start at least.

"This body has shown up out of nowhere. But because this place now houses the rich, I can't be mucking about here."

"Shit always flows down I'm afraid darling."

"Yes, I know. I was raised by you, remember. So, can you just lose the jokes and go down to take a look? It's bad enough, I've got you here. If my boss found out I was letting someone like you wander about a crime scene, then I'd be out on my arse."

Hugh bit his tongue. He was used to the phrase, "someone like him" coming at him from the police. They didn't exactly back his methods and philosophies on the crime in the city, but then neither would he when he was in the police force. But a young Hugh hadn't seen what he had seen now, and neither had Karen, so he let it slide.

"So why call someone like me at all?"

"It's the body. It's just not right," she said, her eyes falling to the stairs, her eyebrows knitting together.

"You think something supernatural caused this?"

Karen's nose wrinkled at the word supernatural.

"I don't know, you are the expert on *that* subject."

She never did like discussing *that* subject, but she had asked him here to help and Hugh wasn't about to pass up the opportunity.

"Ok Karen. I'll go down and take a look for you," he said.

She gave him a sharp nod. "You've got five minutes until the forensic team is back. Make it count."

Hugh descended into what would have been a grand chapel before its hotel lobby style makeover. Oh, the bones of the chapel were still there; the wood panelling had been presevered, the stained-glass windows buffed and shined and the period features in the ceiling repainted. But the room's skin had been given a splash of bland grey and the carpet had all the charm and style of a golf clubhouse.

Still, history had still maintained its presence in the form of a body lying in the centre of the room lit up by four forensic lamps.

Hugh let out a sigh as his hip complained at being put through the ordeal of stairs. His breath floated towards the ceiling in a cloud of white. He hadn't felt cold like this in a while. The snot from his nose felt like it was going to freeze, and his nipples felt like they could cut glass.

It wasn't hard to tell where the source of the cold came from. Frozen solid and covered in icy white crystal, the body in the centre of the room twinkled like Christmas lights under the shine of the forensic lamps.

The body's mouth hung open as if in a permanent scream.

Hugh swallowed. The metallic taste of the supernatural thick in the back of his throat.

"Creepy isn't it."

"Jesus fucking Christ!" bellowed Hugh, staggering to his right. His feet got caught under themselves and, unable to keep his balance, he grabbed for the nearest object—one of the light stands. Light swung wildly across the room, the shadows chasing after it. Hugh swung round the pole like a fat stripper trying to test the limits of its craftsmanship.

He landed on the ground, two of the light stands crashing down next to him, their light pointing to the ceiling. His hip throbbed from the landing.

"What was that noise?" shouted Karen from the top of the stairs.

"Nothing," called Hugh from the floor.

"Are you sure? It sounded pretty loud to me." asked the same well-spoken whispering voice which almost made him shit his pants.

Standing over him was Fanny Archibald. A 15-year-old girl who had been dead since 1865. Blood from a wound in her head smeared across her face and black dress. The wound carved in the front of her skull had come from an errant butcher's cleaver. Much to Hugh's disgust and annoyance, the blade had been removed, leaving the wound to constantly bleed.

She liked to think she was Watson to Hugh's Sherlock. In reality, he was no Sherlock, and at least the great detective didn't have a partner who occasionally terrified him.

"You creepy bitch. I could have had a heart attack."

Fanny beamed, revealing a disgusting set of brown teeth.

"That would have been delightful. One could do with the permanent company."

"No thanks, I see *one* enough and I occasionally enjoy the land of the living. Unless they have whisky where you are?"

Fanny raised her hand to play with a light Hugh hadn't knocked down, but her hand passed straight through.

"No whisky I'm afraid. No tasting food. No feeling of a warm summer breeze on your skin or snowflakes touching one's nose."

"And this is why I wouldn't want to spend any more permanent time with you. You are so bloody dramatic. I've told you before, stop trying to scare me to death to get some company. How about passing across the veil and staying there with the rest of the dead? I'm sure there would be a few pals there waiting for you."

Fanny shook her head vigorously. "A ghastly place. Much more fun here and I get to help you."

Fanny liked to assist by taking the spirits Hugh hunted down and helping them across the veil so they could find peace instead of staying here and being a pain in his backside. Hugh knew he needed her but tried his best never to mention this. He wouldn't want her getting above her station.

"Who is your new friend?"

Hugh turned his head and the tip of his nose almost touched the skin of the frozen body of the victim.

He scuttled back across the floor like a clinically obese spider.

In his haste to get away, he clattered into another spotlight, sending the light flopping over backwards, its light streaking towards the ceiling.

"What was that?" shouted Karen from upstairs.

"Nothing!" called Hugh lying as still as possible and feeling like a teenager who had been caught watching porn by his mother.

"Do you need me to come down?"

"No need!" he shouted, a little too keenly.

"Well, hurry up, and remember, it's a crime scene. You are not supposed to be touching anything."

Hugh thought it best not to respond.

Fanny giggled into her hands.

"Very funny," said Hugh.

With a heave and a few noises reserved only for the most intense types of bending down, Hugh got back to his feet. He found his bowler hat and cane, picking them off the floor before giving himself a pat down, sending dusting particles sparkling across the stream of white light.

Shadows had fallen across the corpse, yet the crystal frost, which kept the body encased in a state frostier than Santa Clause's bawbag, sparkled almost as bright as the lights pointed towards the ceiling.

Hugh had never seen a body like this, and he had seen a lot of weird shit. He lifted one lamp from the ground and shone the light down on the body.

"It's so shiny," said Fanny, her voice a little too excited by the sight of a dead body for Hugh's liking.

But she wasn't wrong. The glare of the light against the white frost covering the body made Hugh blink, the outline of the mummified corpse remaining behind the darkness of his eyelids.

"Can we touch it?" said Fanny, her eyes widening.

"Well, you can't," said Hugh.

"Pig," pouted Fanny.

"What? I am a detective, remember? I deal in facts. And it's a fact that you can't touch this body. Is that not correct Fanny?"

"It's Detective Archibald and yes we both know it is a fact that you are a horrible pig with the touch of an elephant. Just be careful, your daughter did say not to touch anything."

Hugh stood up to his full height, puffed his chest out and tilted his chin skywards.

"Does nobody remember that I was a police officer for thirty bloody years and most of that was as a detective? I've seen more crime scenes and dead bodies than, well, ok, maybe not you but still."

Hugh removed his favourite Mont Blanc pen from the top pocket of his suit and bent down over the frozen corpse.

"Honestly, you would think when you get to my age you are just to have a bullet put in the back of your neck and put down. We are actually useful us old fogies, you know. We do have that thing called, oh I don't know, life experience."

Hugh reached the pen out and jabbed the sparkling surface of the corpse's cheekbone.

The pen immediately broke the surface of the skin. Small cracked lines appeared around the hole where the pen penetrated ice.

Hugh removed the pen quickly from the hole, only to watch in horror as the hole expanded, the cracks surrounding it working their way down the body.

He reached a hand out to stop the ice from breaking, but moved too quickly, his knuckles smashing into the corpse's ribs with a *crack*.

Hugh held his breath, not sure what to do.

Crunch.

The sound echoed around the room.

The corpse immediately turned to dust before Hugh's eyes. Thousands and thousands of specks covering the thick carpet at his feet.

From the dust floated up a wisp of grey smoke.

Hugh's mouth hung open as the smoke spun in the white light of the forensic lamps. A hypnotic movement like the smoke from a blown-out candle. But its elegant movements grew more intense, spinning faster and faster.

Hugh staggered back as the tornado of smoke formed a thick mass. The metallic taste at the back of his mouth became an almost gloopy syrup in his throat. Hugh gaped as a face appeared in the smoke. The face of a stern looking old man with thick eyebrows and a gaunt face.

The apparition opened his mouth to speak, "A disgrace to the name of this institution, that one."

With a withering shake of his head, the man melted into the ether.

Hugh stood blinking down at the mass of white powder on the floor, trying to comprehend what he had just seen.

"Well," said Fanny, "it's lucky we have your experience here, is it not?"

Hugh kept his gaze on the floor. He did not want to see the smug look on her face.

"Is everything ok down there?" shouted Karen from the top of the stair, "the forensic team is coming back. They'll know if you have touched anything, so take care when you come back up."

The next night Hugh sat in silence in the foyer of the apartments. Fanny paced back and forth in front of him, trying to keep quiet, something she found extremely difficult to do.

To fill the silence, she picked at the scab on her forehead. She was always picking at that thing, playing with the blood which oozed out and popping her finger inside like it was some kind of toy.

Hugh checked his peculiar watch. The largest hand followed Fanny as she paced back and forth in front of him. The middle hand spun at the slow pace he was accustomed to when Fanny was around. The smallest hand was not green. Thankfully. Hugh doubted it would stay that way, not after what he saw yesterday.

Lowering his hand, he stared back down the lavish entrance of the building, trying to imagine the hundreds of poor boys and girls running back and forth across this foyer as they moved to their next class. A cacophony of noise, no doubt. Now the entrance was filled with the hostile glare of the concierge sat behind his desk. The weed of a man had not been happy when Hugh politely told him he would be sitting in his entrance for the evening. Apparently, this would "upset the residents who had already been through enough."

Hugh had promptly sat his ample backside down and given the concierge a look, which suggested he would have to drag him out.

But that quiet battle of wills had been hours ago, and now Hugh's hip was burning from sitting in the seat for too long. Too many hours on his arse always made his hip complain. He would never give up sitting for prolonged periods of time, it was his favourite hobby, he just chose comfier seats these days.

Even so, he could do with some movement or something happening, otherwise he was in for a long night. But he would stay here all night if that's what it would take. He had to make it up to Karen.

To say she had been upset at him for destroying her evidence was like saying it rained and got a little windy in Scotland.

"Dad, what am I supposed to tell the full *fucking* forensic team that are on their way back here."

"Er, it was mice?"

"That's a terrible excuse," whispered Fanny, stood next to him. She had, of course, come along to watch Hugh explain himself to Karen—there was no way she would miss out on that level of entertainment.

"Be quiet you," grumbled Hugh.

"Who are you talking to?" asked Karen.

"Oh, it's just Fanny being a smart arse again."

Karen knew about Fanny. He told his daughter a few years ago about his life with the spirits and the "help" Fanny provided. She was one of the few on this side of the veil who knew.

When he told her, she had suggested he put the bottle down. Then she had realised he was being serious and suggested he get some medical attention.

"One is only pointing out how ridiculous your excuse is."

"One thanks you and would like you to politely fuck off."

Karen shook her head. "Dad, I've potentially lost my job and you are standing there pretending to talk to a ghost."

"I'm not pretending. She is really here. I wish she wasn't."

"Charming," said Fanny.

"And I wish I had never called you here," said Karen.

"I'm sorry Karen, I will sort it."

"How? My evidence is a pile of dust on the floor."

"Snow actually," said Fanny.

Hugh glared at Fanny before turning back to Karen. "There was a spirit trapped inside. Someone or something did that to them. If we stake out the building for long enough, we will find it."

"You want me to let you hang around this crime scene longer?"

"Trust me—"

Karen snorted.

"Ok, don't trust me. Just let me fix this. One night is all I ask, me and Fanny will get to the bottom of this, I promise."

"Detective Archibald," said Fanny.

"Don't promise Dad. You've never been good at keeping those."

Hugh drew in a breath at that jab. The girl knew how to cut deep, she learned that from him.

"Please Karen, let me fix this," he said, making eye contact with eyes which made him feel like he was staring into his own reflection.

Karen stared back, long and hard. "One night. Then I'll clean up your mess like always."

"Oh, such fun!" Fanny had said, clapping her hands together.

Now the novelty had worn off for the spirit.

"This is so boring," she said, pacing in front of him in the foyer. "When is something going to happen?"

"For someone who spends her eternity floating about on this side of the veil you would think you would be used to being bored."

"One usually finds better company to spend time with."

"Well, why don't you go and bother them."

"Oh, you are such a misery guts aren't you."

"And you are an insufferably annoying cun—"

A green glow filled the foyer, cutting Hugh off mid insult.

He looked at his watch. The smallest hand lit up a poisonous shade of green. The middle hand spun like a waltzer at the fairground and the longest hand pointed down the corridor past the concierge.

"Looks like you are going to get a show after all," said Hugh, grabbing hold of his cane and humphing himself out of his seat.

"Excellent, one does like a good show," said Fanny as she followed him past the frowning concierge.

"Excuse me sir, where do you think you are going?"

"To cause a disturbance," said Hugh, not looking back.

***

Hugh limped as fast as his gammy leg would take him, grunting and wheezing with each step. A few feet in front of him strode Fanny, looking back every few steps to roll her eyes at his lack of pace.

Lucky for you. You are dead. You don't need to live in constant pain.

The building was a maze of corridors which were too long for Hugh's liking.

But his watch kept them right. It always did. The large hand twisting and turning with corridors.

Left.

Right.

Another left.

Meanwhile, the middle hand spun faster and faster until it was nothing but a circle of black on the green face of the watch.

Their last right-hand turn stopped Hugh and Fanny outside a glass door.

Peering in through the glass, Hugh could see some kind of bar. Comfortable looking leather armchairs and various shades of boring yet tasteful blues had been used to decorate the space. Hugh cursed at not picking one of those comfortable looking chairs to park his backside in earlier. He could have rested his hip and enjoyed a drink whilst he waited.

The bar was empty now, the residents long since retiring to their apartments. Nothing but Hugh's heartbeat filled the silence and Fanny scratching at the wound on her forehead, of course.

Hugh stood outside, catching his breath, and mopping his brow.

As they ventured deeper into the building, the metallic taste at the back of his mouth had grown thicker. But now, standing outside the room, it felt as if he were sucking on a handful of pennies.

Fanny stood behind him, scratching at her scab.

"Are we going in?" she asked.

Hugh swallowed. "How about you first?"

"Oh, how brave and gentlemanly of you."

"I'm not brave or a gentleman."

"And I am not going in first."

Hugh sighed. "Fine, but at some point, you are going to remind me why you are here."

"My sparkling conversation."

Hugh grunted and reached down to the door handle and tried to ignore the shaking in his hand.

The handle was ice cold and almost sticky, like it had been sitting outside in the height of winter. He knew if he pressed his tongue to the handle it would stick, but he supposed if you go around licking door handles, you get what you deserve.

Holding his breath, he turned the handle and pushed the door open.

A loud creak filled the silence. The darkness inside the room was thick and uninviting.

Hugh stood waiting for something to happen. A ghost to appear, to jump out and scare the crap out of him; they tended to do that, the creepy bastards.

"Are we going in or are we just going to stand here all evening?" asked Fanny impatiently.

"I'm working my way up to it."

"It's empty. What is there to worry about?"

Hugh raised a bushy grey eyebrow in Fanny's direction.

"You know that's not how your lot work."

Fanny frowned back at him, the gesture causing the wound on her forehead to pucker open.

"You know I don't like you using the term, "your lot." We were all like you once." Fanny looked him up and down. "Well, maybe not all of us. Some of us were less—solid."

"I do apologise. I will stick to calling you Fanny or creepy bitch from now on."

Satisfied the room had been quiet for long enough, Hugh took a tentative step inside. And instantly regretted it.

The room tilted. Not a full-blown spin but enough to make Hugh groan, close his eyes and lean on his cane, hoping the couple of packets of crisps on a roll he had eaten for tea held in his stomach. The concierge would hate if he spewed on his carpet.

When he regained control of his stomach, he opened his eyes to find they were no longer alone.

Rows of hard wooden school desks had replaced the comfortable armchairs. The thick wool of the carpet was now a dusty-looking floor, and the bar had transformed into a large blackboard. In front of which, his back to Hugh and Fanny, stood a tall man in black robes.

He was writing on the board, the chalk squeaking painfully with each word he wrote. His deep voice boomed out across the room.

"And who can tell me the English equivalent of the following Latin phrase?" The word *cogitatio* appeared on the board.

Reflection. Hugh was old enough to remember the horrors of being taught Latin at school.

The teacher (for that's what Hugh presumed he must be), spun almost ballerina like away from the board to face out to the room. His gaze was calculated and sinister, like he was a predator searching for his next victim.

A grin spread across his face, folding his skin into wrinkles.

He had found his victim.

The only seat filled in the room was by a boy who must have been about ten or eleven. His hair stuck up on end and he was dressed in a scruffy hand-me-down looking blazer with gold buttons, an off-white shirt and stained looking school shorts. He sat with his head bowed, clearly trying to avoid the gaze of his teacher.

Kind of difficult when you are the only one in the class.

"Anderson," called the teacher.

The boy flinched in his seat like he had been struck but remained silent and curled himself further down like a mouse trying to hide from the house cat.

"I say Anderson. I call your name therefore you respond."

The boy looked up but said nothing.

The teacher took a step forward.

"I am addressing you, boy. Address me as is expected of this institution, or are you above the rules?"

"Oh, let's go sit down and join the class," said Fanny, her voice full of childish excitement. She skipped ahead of Hugh and slipped into the desk next to the boy.

Hugh's legs were planted in place and the hairs on the back of his neck stood up.

The teacher stepped closer to the young boy called Anderson, a wooden cane sliding out from underneath the arm of his robe.

Hugh did not like where this was going.

"Anderson, are you going to respond to me or are am I going to have to teach you a lesson in front of this class again?"

The teacher loomed over Anderson now.

Fanny turned and gave Hugh a large grin as if they were both VIP spectators at a first-class show.

"Well boy?"

Anderson lifted his head.

Hugh stepped further into the room so he could get a better look at the boy's eyes. They were blue and vibrant and staring deep into his teachers.

Far too blue and vibrant for anyone dead.

The boy grinned, saliva drooling out of his mouth and down his chin. His teacher flinched and took a step back, as did Hugh.

Before the teacher could move too far away, Anderson lunged forward and grabbed hold of his hands, pinning them to the table.

"Anderson, unhand me at once," yelped the teacher.

The boy stood, a wicked smile spread across his face caused white foam to dribble down his chin and onto the desk where it melted away.

The teacher leaned back, trying to get as far away from the boy in front of him. Hugh couldn't blame him, he was contemplating turning and running back up the corridor, out the building and across the field to the nearest pub.

But the teacher was going nowhere, and neither was Hugh; his legs seemed to have stopped working.

The teacher thrashed like a trapped animal; his eyes wide as he searched the room for help.

"Children help your teacher, please!" he cried.

"No!" shouted Fanny before cackling an evil laugh. She really could be an evil bitch when she wanted to.

Anderson leaned in, opening his mouth wide. The inside of his mouth was pitch black yet moving, like there was a black snake squirming where his tongue should have been.

"Call the headmaster children! Get help!" The teacher bucked away from the horrors inside Anderson's mouth, his hair now a wild mess.

"Call him yourself!" shouted Fanny, leaning back in her chair and putting her feet up on the desk in front, revealing a pair of bare feet covered in scabs.

Anderson let out a rattling breath, like a pinball being shaken inside a tin can. A cloud of white smoke blew from his mouth straight into the face of the teacher.

The man immediately stopped shouting; his face instead contorted in a silent scream as the cloudy breath froze him in place. The white wormed its way across the teacher's skin, encasing him in a coffin of sparkling frost.

The boy released his teacher's hands and closed his mouth, his task complete.

The mummified white statue fell to the ground, arms out, his white face still open in a scream.

"Bravo, what a show!" whooped Fanny, clapping her hands enthusiastically.

The boy turned his head and trained his blue eyes on Hugh.

***

"Now easy their laddie," said Hugh, holding up a shaking hand.

But the boy wasn't listening to him. He snarled and moved towards Hugh; his blue eyes never wavered.

Hugh backed his way out of the door.

The boy opened his mouth and for a moment Hugh expected to be covered in a cloud of white, a voiceless scream leaving his mouth as he was mummified in a casing of frozen glass.

Instead the boy spoke, his voice a rattling murmur, "Leave...me...alone."

Hugh was tempted to take him up on that offer. But then he had promised Karen he would deal with this problem. Of course, he promised this before he knew a ghost which blasted ice from its mouth would be involved.

"I can't leave you alone, but I can help you. If you just sit down, we can have a chat and see if we can fix it?" said Hugh, aware of how much his voice shook as he spoke.

"Maybe have some tea as well," said Fanny, who had slinked her way next to Hugh.

"Tea?" whispered Hugh out of the side of his mouth.

"Yes, tea. Tea always seemed to help adults when I was alive. They even had a cup after they found my body, all standing around chatting, sipping their tea whilst I lay dead on the floor. Quiet callus, now I think about it."

Anderson growled as he stepped closer.

"Somehow I don't think tea is going to fucking work this time."

"Leave," moaned Anderson.

Hugh and Fanny backed up into the hall.

The boy opened his mouth wide—the black sickness inside twisted and for a moment Hugh stood frozen to the spot, staring at its unholy movement.

Then Anderson let out a loud, rattling breath. A cloud of white emerged deep from within the boy.

Hugh lunged forward; his cane extended. He hooked the cane onto the door handle and pulled.

The door slammed shut just in time for the cloud of white to meet the glass panels and turn them to frost, blocking the view of the monster within.

Replacing the view into the room, Hugh stared back at himself wide eyed, his moustache covered in white flakes of snow where the cloud of white had managed to touch him.

Stood next to him was a young girl, her black hair shiny and vibrant, her eyes a bright green, her skin a milky white. Fanny's eyes widened and she let out a scream.

Hugh turned to his left to see Fanny cower. The ghost with the blood covered wound in her head, the wild black hair, the gaunt face.

He realised the frosted glass had turned into a mirror and reflected what she had been.

A scream came from the classroom. The boy had clearly seen his own reflection.

Hugh reached a hand for Fanny's shoulder, but it passed straight through.

The girl in the reflection had been solid, vibrant, and full of colour.

Alive.

Not the girl Hugh had tried to comfort.

"Are you ok?" asked Hugh.

Fanny let out a whimper, her hands covering her face.

"I'm dead," said Fanny.

Well, yes, thought Hugh, but didn't say it. Fanny, of course, knew this before she saw her reflection, but the reality of a ghost's situation on this side of the veil was always one step away in their mind until they were forced to look in a mirror.

So not that different from the living.

"It's ok, you are perfectly fine the way you are," said Hugh, trying to reassure the dead girl.

"I am hideous."

"No, you are not, you are—"

"Dead," she wailed.

Hugh chose his next words carefully. "And thank goodness you are, then I wouldn't have met you and be able to call you a friend."

"Do you mean that?" said Fanny, sliding her hands from her face and smiling at Hugh, revealing her hideously stained teeth. A spider crawled from beneath her top lip and worked its way along her gums, crawling up the side of her cheek and disappearing into the gaping wound in her forehead.

Hugh began to gag, but the smashing of glass cut him off.

He raised his arms just in time as hundreds of shards covered him, nipping at his hands and cheeks.

Lowering his hands, he found one of the comfortable leather chairs from the residents' bar lying at his feet.

A growl came from the classroom. The boy glowered at them through the shattered glass door.

"Oh hello, I forgot you were there," said Fanny.

"Run!" shouted Hugh, turning away from the boy and the classroom and began limping up the corridor.

"Oh fun, a chase!" said Fanny, swooping next to him.

A loud snarl came from behind Hugh as he pushed through a heavy wooden door. Hugh's hip screamed as he hurried forward, not once looking back.

Fanny giggled next to him.

Through another door they went, slamming it behind them. Another roar came from behind as the boys' breath missed its target.

Hugh slid to a halt at the end of a junction, trying to remember the way.

"Where are we going?" asked Fanny.

"Back to the other reception room." Hugh said. He had an idea of how to stop Anderson but needed what was in the room.

"Oh, was that left, or right? One does not recall."

"Yeah, I gathered that."

"He is quite close, you know."

Hugh turned to see the boy's face appearing through the last door Hugh had slammed behind him, his snarling head floating by itself at waist height.

He smiled at Hugh as he crawled fully through the door on all fours, drool cascading from his mouth like a daemon dog.

Hugh grunted and turned left.

"Is this the right way?" asked Fanny as she ran next to him.

The boy's rattling breath filled the corridor as he closed in on them.

Hugh took another right. Then a left.

A blast of cold air hit his shoulder as he turned the corner just in time. The frost travelling down his left arm made his fingers tips feel numb.

For a moment, he thought he had a stroke. At his age, that wasn't out of the question, although the timing would have been unfortunate.

He stared down at his hand, shaking away the frost crawling across his skin, his fingers turning blue and his breath coming in sharp shallow gasps.

Hugh staggered forward, but the floor beneath his feet had disappeared.

"Watch out for the—," cried Fanny.

Hugh let out a cry as he toppled forward, the thickly carpeted stairs hurtling towards him. The first blow hit him on the shoulder, replacing the numb feeling in his arm from the frost with a jolting stab of pain. The second bounce off the stairs caught him in the ribs, pushing the breath from his lungs. The third landed on his hip—the bad hip. Hugh briefly got to see a couple of black spots across his vision from that blow.

He scraped to a carpet burning halt at the bottom of the stairs, his cane and bowler hat rolling away from him.

"I was trying to say watch out for the stairs," said Fanny, her hideous face appearing above him.

A growl from the top of the stairs drowned Hugh's groan out.

No rest for the wicked.

Rocking himself onto his back, Hugh rolled over to find the boy's shimmering blue eyes staring down at him.

"Persistent bastard this one," said Hugh, getting to his knees. His head swam from the pain, but he gritted his teeth and focused on standing. The boy had to get a full view of the room for this to work.

Fanny whimpered as she realised what was happening and ducked behind Hugh.

"Come on down Anderson," called Hugh.

The boy bounded down the stairs on his gangly limbs, his mouth opened, the black sickness within squirming, desperate to get out.

Hugh stood his ground.

Anderson dove into the room with a roar, then slammed to a halt, falling onto his backside and yelping.

He stared wide eyed at the mirrored wall behind Hugh. A scream left his mouth so loud Hugh half expected the mirror to shatter. But the glass held firm, and the boy clawed at his face as he stared at his own reflection.

Hugh stole a glance over his shoulder. In the reflection, a boy in a school uniform sat on the floor in front of Hugh and a girl in black cowered behind him. His own thinning grey hair was wild, white powder covered his left arm and his face was grey from the pain covering his body.

The boy's knees were curled up under his chin and his arms hugged them close. He stared out of the mirror at Hugh with the look of someone with experience well above his junior years. Those were the eyes of a boy who had endured too much, too young.

Hugh looked towards the cowering, moaning version of the boy at his feet. The little boy in the mirror was inside that thing. He wanted out and just wanted to go home. But the only way to rescue him was through the mirror, and only one person could do that.

"Fanny, are you ok?"

The girl whimpered a response.

"I need your help."

She didn't respond, for once she had lost her voice.

"I need you to go into the mirror and help the boy across the veil."

"No—"

Hugh turned to face Fanny.

She had her head in her hands.

"Come on Fanny. He's just a little boy. Look at him."

"No, I can't look. I can't look at myself."

"You don't have to, just look at the boy."

Fanny hesitated, scratching frantically at her face.

"Come on. You just need to step in, and grab hold of his hand, simple as that. I'll be here watching."

Fanny shook her head like a puppy dog.

The beast behind Hugh was whimpering.

"He's just lost Fanny. Just like all the others you help save. He needs you to save him."

"But I look hideous."

Hugh leaned in closer to Fanny.

"That's who you were, not who you are now. You are a different person now and I see nothing hideous about you."

A spider which had been nesting somewhere in Fanny's hair chose that moment to scuttle out from its hiding place across her forehead and into the open wound.

Hugh gulped down the taste of bile. Those creepy little buggers seemed to just wait for him to give Fanny a compliment to appear.

"This boy wants to be just like you. He no longer wants to be trapped inside this thing behind me. He wants to move on and only you can help him, Fanny."

"Detective Archibald," sniffed Fanny.

Hugh smiled. "Detective Archibald, of course."

She raised her head and looked into Hugh's eyes, her own wide and glassy.

"Ok, I'll do it."

"Good lass. Just step in and chat to him, see if he will move over the veil."

Fanny let out a shuddering breath and turned to face the mirror. She kept her eyes on the boy, never wavering toward her own reflection, and took a step forward.

Hugh felt his chest tighten as she stepped up to the mirror and waved at the boy. For a moment he wanted to call her back, worried if she stepped in, she would be gone forever.

Another girl lost.

But he held strong.

Anderson stared at her through the mirror before raising a hand to give her a tentative wave.

Fanny waved back and took another deep breath. She stepped into the mirror, the glass quivering like a disturbed pond.

Hugh watched her kneel next to the boy and whisper into his ear. The two of them almost looked like brother and sister and Hugh felt like he was spying on them sharing a great secret he wasn't allowed to hear.

The Anderson at his feet let out another cry of anguish.

Inside the mirror, the dead teenage girl and the dead boy stood and faced Hugh. They both smiled at Hugh and interlocked hands.

Hugh smiled back and nodded at Fanny. She had been brave.

The beast at Hugh's feet tried to rise, but it was too late. The girl and the boy faded from the mirror.

One last scream ripped through the hall as the beast crumbled, shattering into thousands of tiny pieces, its hostage finally free.

Detective Hugh McRath sat on a bench outside the apartments wrapped up in a thick overcoat to protect himself from the early morning chill. The skies were clear, and the sun was trying its best to melt away the frost covering the field in front of the former school. Hugh's breath came out in clouds of white, reminding him of the monster chasing him last night. With a wince, he pulled his overcoat tighter round himself. The fall down the stairs made it painful to even blink this morning, and he was already looking forward to a day of painkillers and whisky.

His daughter (or DI Karen Dunn) sat on the opposite side of the bench. Hugh noted this was as far away from him as was humanly possible. She still looked tired, the bags under her eyes heavier than the night before, and her hair scraped back off her face. But Hugh could still see his little girl under the passing of time and stress.

She was a mirror into his past mistakes. The drinking. His disappearance into the supernatural world. Her Mother.

Every line and wrinkle a reminder of where he had ended up. Hugh's heart swelled at being able to finally sit next to his daughter (no matter the distance) but it also ached from the memories.

Beyond the iron fence at the bottom of the field, the early morning traffic rumbled past, filling the silence between father and daughter.

Hugh shifted on the bench.

"So, how do you explain this to the higher ups? Your old dad coming to save the day."

Karen frowned, not looking in his direction.

"I certainly won't be using that in my explanation. Anyway, it should be easy. There is no body anymore. Thanks to you."

"You're welcome."

"And there definitely won't be any more bodies, right?"

"Correct. The boy has gone across the veil."

Karen's frown thickened.

"And why was he hanging about here again?"

"He was trapped inside a version of himself which was feeding on his anger."

"Sounds like Eve when she is throwing one of her tantrums."

"I'd love to see one of her tantrums."

"Why was this boy so angry?" asked Karen, ignoring Hugh's attempt at reconciliation.

"I'm not sure. He was an orphan back when this was a school. It's possible he wasn't treated how he wanted to be?"

"And the body?"

"One of his old teacher's I am guessing."

"Jeez, who'd be a teacher. And what made this boy leave?"

"He saw his reflection. He saw what he used to be. The dead don't like to be reminded of what they have become. It hurts them too much."

Karen didn't respond to this, instead staring off across the glistening field.

Hugh wanted to pry more into her life, but just being able to sit next to his daughter right now was a step further towards redemption than he had been in a long time.

"Sitting here with you just now reminds me of when we used to go to Inverleith Park and feed the ducks. Do you remember that? We used to feed the ducks and then we'd sit on the bench, share a sandwich and a packet of crisps."

"I remember," said Karen, "you fell asleep once as you were so hungover, and I had to sit for an hour in silence next to you."

Just like that, the memory turned to ash in Hugh's mind.

Hugh tutted. "I wasn't always—"

Karen stood, turning to Hugh, and gave him a nod.

"Thanks for your help."

Formality had returned, she was DI Dunn again. Hugh felt the opportunity to bridge the gap between them slipping through his fingers.

"Anytime. It was nice to see you. I'd love to—"

"You have a good day Dad."

Hugh closed his mouth and nodded at his daughter.

Karen took one more glance in Hugh's direction, sighed, then walked away towards her parked car.

Hugh watched her go, trying to ignore the urge to call after her.

At least she had called him Dad.

"It's a start at least," whispered a chilling voice in Hugh's right ear.

Hugh yelped and slid down the bench, catching himself before he landed on the wet grass at his feet.

Heart racing, he looked to his right to see Fanny, sat uncomfortably close to him, a grin on her face.

Hugh straightened himself up on the bench and adjusted his bowler hat.

"Listening in, were you?"

"One is always listening."

"Creep."

Fanny sniggered.

Hugh kept his gaze ahead but asked, "Do you think so?"

"Think what?"

"That it's a start?" he said, nodding toward Karen's car, which trundled down the long entrance towards the main road.

"Oh yes, she is warming to you. I mean, how could one not given your heart," said Fanny, fluttering her eyes at Hugh and attempting to dust off the shoulder of his jacket, her scabbed hand passing through.

"Very good," laughed Hugh, "well, we shall see how long it takes for me to cock it up again."

Hugh turned in his seat to face Fanny. "And, how are you?"

"You want to know how I am doing?" asked Fanny, putting her hand to her chest. A spider skittered out from the sleeve of her dress before disappearing into her hair.

"Yes, you. I've got a heart, remember? How are you after what you saw in there?" said Hugh, nodding to the building behind them.

"Oh. One is fine," said Fanny, but she lowered her gaze and played with the folds of the skirt of her frock.

Hugh pursed his lips. He knew how difficult it must have been for Fanny to see herself in the mirror and still step through to help Anderson. Maybe for once he should compliment her.

"You did good," said Hugh, "we make a good team, us two. When you listen."

"I knew you thought that even though you never say it," said Fanny, looking up at Hugh, a wide grin on her face revealing her hideous teeth.

"Yeah, well—"

"It is excellent news!"

"Why?" said Hugh frowning, instantly regretting his decision to be nice to the dead girl.

Fanny clapped her hands together. "Because I have made a new friend who needs our help."

Hugh groaned.

Enjoy this book?

You can make a difference. Honest reviews of my books help bring them to the attention of other readers.

If you've enjoyed this book I would be very grateful if you could spare a few minutes to leave a review (it can be as short as you like) on the site from which you purchased the book.

Thank you very much.

About the author

Scott Williamson is a Scottish writer who does not have the attention span to write in one genre, so plans to write in them all. All of his stories have a twist of Scottish cheek, a nip of darkness and a sprinkle of hope. Scott lives in Auld Reekie Edinburgh with his wife and three kids. When he is not in his writing cage fighting with the blank page, he is curled up and broken on the couch after a day parenting his tearaway children.

Want to stay in touch?

Scott loves to hear from readers, his website below has details of how to get in touch or drop him a message on Instagram (@scott_williamson_author).

www.scottwilliamsonauthor.com

www.ingramcontent.com/pod-product-compliance
Lightning Source LLC
Chambersburg PA
CBHW021732190726
48288CB00009B/3022